Nasrudin
Travels With Nasrudin
The Misadventures of the Mystifying Nasrudin
The Peregrinations of the Perplexing Nasrudin
The Voyages and Vicissitudes of Nasrudin

Stories
The Arabian Nights Adventures
Scorpion Soup
Tales Told to a Melon
The Afghan Notebook
The Man Who Found Himself
The Caravanserai Stories
The Mysterious Musings of Clementine Fogg

Miscellaneous
The Reason to Write
Zigzag Think
Being Myself

Research
Cultural Research
The Middle East Bedside Book
Three Essays

Anthologies
The Anthologies
The Clockmaker's Box
Tahir Shah Fiction Reader
Tahir Shah Travel Reader

Edited by
Congress With a Crocodile
A Son of a Son, Volume I
A Son of a Son, Volume II
The Moroccan Anthologies

Screenplays
Casablanca Blues: The Screenplay
Timbuctoo: The Screenplay

THE VOYAGES
AND VICISSITUDES
OF NASRUDIN

TAHIR SHAH

THE VOYAGES
AND VICISSITUDES
OF NASRUDIN

TAHIR SHAH

MMXXI

Secretum Mundi Publishing Ltd
Kemp House
City Road
London
EC1V 2NX
United Kingdom

www.secretum-mundi.com
info@secretum-mundi.com

First published by Secretum Mundi Publishing Ltd, 2021
VERSION [12052021]

THE VOYAGES AND VICISSITUDES OF NASRUDIN

© TAHIR SHAH

Tahir Shah asserts the right to be identified as the Author of the Work in
accordance with the Copyright, Designs and Patents Act 1988.
A CIP catalogue record for this title is available from the British Library.

Visit the author's website at:

Tahirshah.com

ISBN 978-1-912383-80-1

For Alexander Maitland,
with affection

CONTENTS

KIRKUK
IRAQ

In No Time

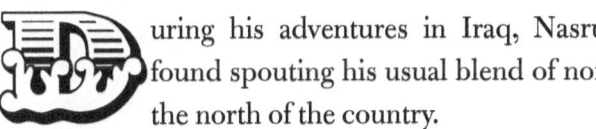 uring his adventures in Iraq, Nasrudin was found spouting his usual blend of nonsense in the north of the country.

As they didn't have many wise fool travellers passing through, the people there developed an interest in him. It wasn't long before he was invited on the local television channel to talk about his life and adventures.

Halfway through the TV appearance, Nasrudin was asked how much time he planned to spend in Iraq. He looked flummoxed at the question.

'But everyone knows that time doesn't exist,' he said earnestly.

The interviewer flinched.

'Of course it does.'

'No it doesn't.'

'Well, if time doesn't exist, why are you wearing a wristwatch, which appears to be set to the correct time?'

Nasrudin swished a hand through the air, as though the question was beneath him.

'I said *time* does not exist,' he answered curtly. 'I never claimed wristwatches don't exist!'

BEIJING
CHINA

Sharing Upwards

While touring the Forbidden City, Nasrudin spotted a party official sitting alone in the shade.

Without giving it a moment's thought, he strode over to him.

Calling greetings, the wise fool handed the official the empty coffee cup he was holding, exchanging it for the cup the man was about to drink.

Then, removing his moth-eaten old jacket, he swapped it for the official's overcoat.

After that, Nasrudin took off his filthy old scarf, wound it around the man's neck, and helped himself to his pristine silk scarf.

Enraged, the party official demanded to know what the foreigner was doing.

'Those are *my* things!' he barked. 'You have no right to swap them with yours!'

Nasrudin frowned quizzically.

'But I thought communism was about sharing.'

'It is!'

The wise fool shrugged.

'So that's what I'm doing. I'm sharing.'

'No it isn't! You're exchanging rubbish with our good quality stuff!'

Nasrudin leaned back on his heels.

'You may think of it like that,' he said courteously, 'but the way I see it, I am merely sharing upwards.'

AKSUM
ETHIOPIA

Fake Ark

n his travels in Damascus, Nasrudin was sold a large key that he had spotted in an antiques shop in the bazaar.

From the first moment he set eyes on the rusted iron object, he'd been transfixed by it.

Immediately, the shopkeeper had sidled up.

'Your highness has the most excellent taste,' he'd crooned. 'Out of all the objects in my shop, that's by far the most exceptional.'

Gloating, Nasrudin had basked in the praise.

'If this is the key, where is the lock?'

The shopkeeper had sighed.

'Believe it or not, it's the key to the Ark of the Covenant.'

'Where is that?'

'In the north of Ethiopia, at a small city called Aksum.'

Having made a beeline to the city, the wise fool hunted down the building where the Ark of the Covenant was kept, the great iron key in hand.

'I'd like to see the Ark, please,' he said politely.

'Impossible! We show it to no one!' the guard answered.

'But I am the owner of the Ark of the Covenant!'

The guard did a double take.

'I find that very hard to believe,' he said.

Standing as tall as he could manage, Nasrudin forced out his chest to appear far grander than he was.

'If I am not the owner of the Ark, then how can you explain the fact that I have the key?'

The guard conferred with one of the priests and, before Nasrudin knew it, the guardian of the Ark was standing in front of him. Intrigued, he beckoned the foreigner towards him.

'Bring your key,' he whispered.

A moment later, the key was slipped into the lock on the side of the Ark. But however hard Nasrudin tried, it wouldn't turn.

'It's a fake!' the guardian snapped sternly.

His pride dented, Nasrudin waved the key threateningly at the Ark, then at the guardian.

'It's not my key that's phoney!' he roared. 'It's your Ark that's the fake!'

LOS ANGELES
CALIFORNIA

Fast Fiction

Nasrudin started writing romantic novels, and wrote them faster than anyone else alive.

Sometimes he would dictate ten novels at the same time to a bevy of typists.

No one could understand how he managed to write, or rather, dictate, so fast.

Plucking up courage, one of the typists asked the wise fool once her shift had ended.

'Well, I have two pools of stuff in my head. One is filled with characters and the other is filled with plots. What I do is like cooking... I take a pinch of characters and a pinch of plot and mix them together. Then, hey presto! Yet another novel emerges into the world!'

'Do you ever deviate from your system?' the typist asked.

'If the story is too bland, I add a little salt or pepper, but no, no, no, I never deviate.'

The next week, Nasrudin ramped up production, producing five novels a day, and twenty on the weekend. Extra secretaries were hired and, even then, they could hardly keep up.

Exasperated at the lightning speed of creation, the same typist as before asked how the wise fool had managed to increase his output so stupendously.

Looking her in the eye, he smiled, and said:

'Fast food.'

BALKH
AFGHANISTAN

Brain Reformat

Everyone in town was amazed when Nasrudin entered a memory competition.

After all, he was celebrated as a fool, and fools were not expected to possess much grey matter.

The contest required the would-be memory champions to memorize ten thousand pages of Wikipedia. Remarkably, the wise fool managed to get every single question directed to him completely correct.

At the end of the contest, he was asked how he'd managed to beat everyone else.

'Unlike the other participants,' he said, 'I didn't have any other material on my internal hard drive. So there was no limit to the number of pages I could download into my head.'

LONDON
ENGLAND

Ahead of the Trend

asrudin was strolling down Old Bond Street thinking of nothing in particular when, in the window of a leading gallery, he noticed the most beautiful object he'd ever seen.

Unable to contain himself, the wise fool rushed inside and pointed to a painting in a resplendent gilded frame.

'I must have it at any price!' he cried.

The owner of the gallery swanned up, expressing delight in meeting a customer with a rare eye.

'It's one of his early works, of course,' he crooned. 'The way he played with light is quite extraordinary.'

The wise fool frowned.

'I'm not talking about that hideous painting,' he snapped, 'but rather the frame surrounding it.'

The gallery owner assumed the customer was making a joke at his expense, and was about to throw him out. But Nasrudin pleaded to be permitted to buy the gilded frame.

Taking it home, he hung it on a wall and stared at it adoringly.

Although glorious, it was missing something.

So, next day, the wise fool zigzagged through the city in search of the perfect frame with which to frame his frame.

After hours of searching, he came to a frame shop in an old Victorian railway arch. The place had been recommended by half a dozen frame connoisseurs elsewhere.

'Can you frame this masterpiece for me?' he asked.

The framer unwrapped the frame.

'This is a frame, but where's the picture?'

'No, no, I'd like you to frame my frame.'

'But frames don't have frames.'

'This one will.'

The framer took the measurements and spat out a price.

'Are you quite certain that's what you want, sir?' he asked.

The wise fool nodded eagerly.

'Framing frames is likely to become a craze,' he said. 'You see, I'm always ahead of the trend.'

UMM BADR
SUDAN

Reminding the Sky

asrudin was seen in the desert by a passing tribesman, prancing, dancing, and spitting at the ground.

After extensive greetings, the tribesman asked what the foreigner was doing, acting in such a peculiar manner.

'The sky hasn't made rain in so long it's apparently forgotten,' said the wise fool, 'so I'm simply reminding it how to rain.'

MINSK
BELARUS

Lost Marble

In the dead of night, Nasrudin was discovered under the president's bed.

'What the hell are you doing there?!' the dictator bellowed.

'Ah, there it is,' the wise fool answered whimsically.

'*What* is?'

Clambering out of his hiding place, Nasrudin held up a glass marble between thumb and forefinger.

'I've been looking for this everywhere.'

The president of the republic scowled at the intruder.

'You have ten seconds to explain yourself before the armed guards get here and haul you away!'

'Well,' Nasrudin explained with a sigh, 'you know how it is.'

'How what is?'

'How life is! I was playing with my little marble on the other side of the city, when it fell onto the ground and rolled along, and up and down, until it had reached the Independence Palace… Rolling through the great iron gates, it slipped past the guards and into the vast reception area. Then… it rolled up the stairs, left, right, left, along the corridors, into your bedroom, and under the bed.'

'I don't believe a word of it!' the dictator yelled.

'What a shame,' Nasrudin replied meekly, 'because it was such a promising story.'

KABALEBO
SURINAME

The Termites

Although an experienced traveller, and a veteran when it came to being a wise fool, Nasrudin had not swallowed a polar bear before, and so had no inkling of the havoc the creature would wreak on his body and mind.

Within an hour of ingesting the great white mammal, the wise fool was getting hot and cold flushes, palpitations, and had a high-pitched whirring noise ringing in his ears.

As luck would have it, a passing environmentalist had the answer to how to deal with the polar bear.

'Go straight to Suriname,' she said, 'and eat your body weight in termites.'

'Termites?'

The environmentalist nodded.

'And make sure to swallow some water as well, because they dry you out like nothing else.'

Offering sincerest thanks, Nasrudin tramped southwards to the closest cluster of igloos, and then worked out a route to faraway Suriname.

Six weeks after swallowing the polar bear, the wise fool arrived at Kabalebo, where the world's most ferocious termites were said to live in towering mounds.

Getting down on his belly, which was swollen and raw, he opened his mouth extra wide, and waited.

Within ten seconds, a phalanx of termites marched down Nasrudin's tongue, into his mouth, and into the darkness at the back of his throat.

Biding his time until an appropriate quantity of the termites had trooped on in, the wise fool jumped up, whooped boisterously, and yelled:

'To work, boys! There's feasting to be done!'

MEXICO CITY
MEXICO

King of the Queue Bargers

asrudin was a self-proclaimed champion of queue barging – so much so that he started the World Queue Barging Competition to show off his skill to others.

Candidates arrived from all over the world to a rented auditorium in Mexico City and began lining up obediently to file their papers.

Scoffing at their respect for authority, Nasrudin barged to the front.

Then, during the queue barging championships, he barged in front during all the qualifying heats – even when he wasn't supposed to be in a bout of barging.

Rather than being horrified by his uncouth behaviour, all the other candidates applauded.

In awe of the wise fool's barging technique, the judges crowned him 'International King of Queue Bargers'.

The runner-up, a soft-spoken queue barger from Kazakhstan, asked the world champion how he'd got into queue barging in the first place.

Clutching the trophy – sculpted in the form of a golden elbow – Nasrudin regarded his fellow competitor for a moment.

'The first time I remember queue barging,' he said, 'was when I elbowed my twin brother out of the way so I could be the first out of the womb!'

LOS ANGELES
CALIFORNIA

Driverless Car

As a foreigner with no friends, Nasrudin had a habit of taking long taxi rides solely so he could chat to the driver.

The way he saw it, the cost of the ride was well worth it, as he got to air his views on everything – from the situation of the world to the state of the roads.

One day, with nothing else to do, the wise fool ordered a taxi from an app, and was horrified to find it had no driver at all.

'How am I supposed to chitchat to you?' he asked once inside the vehicle.

Silence.

'I said… How am I supposed to chitchat with you?' he repeated.

The car didn't respond.

Clenching his hands into fists, Nasrudin shook them at the dashboard.

'What have things come to,' he hollered, 'when a passenger is forced to talk to himself?!'

CAMBRIDGE
ENGLAND

Guinness World Records

asrudin was hoping to get a job in the prestigious university as a laboratory technician – a role for which he was terribly unqualified.

By chance, he heard that the chief of the department was a huge fan of *Guinness World Records*. Hoping to impress her, he dropped everything he was doing, and did his best to break a record.

First, he bought a pogo-stick and tried jumping up and down in a marathon session – but he couldn't go for more than a few minutes.

Next, he bought a thousand packs of playing cards and did his best to build the world's biggest playing-card house. But, despite many attempts, the structure collapsed after ten cards were in place.

Next, he tried swimming lengths of the local pool. But after a length and a half he caught a cramp and had to stop.

The one thing he was actually good at – remaining silent – may have got him a Guinness Record. But, unfortunately, ten minutes into his feat of prolonged silence, his phone rang and, without thinking, he answered it.

A week after starting out to get a world record, the wise fool's friend asked how he was getting on.

'You might think that I would be depressed,' he replied, a glint in his eye, 'but, on the contrary, I'm excited!'

'And why may I ask is that?'

'Because,' Nasrudin confided, 'I've got a plan.'

A few days slipped by, and the judge from *Guinness World Records* arrived at the auditorium the wise fool had rented, along with the world's media.

Amid a sea of reporters, all of whom had been lured by hyperbole, and plain untruths, Nasrudin made his announcement.

'After many years of tireless work,' he began, 'I have designed and built the world's smallest microscope.'

'Where is it?' a journalist called out.

'There, under that black cloth.'

The Guinness judge appeared as interested as the media.

'Could I take a look?' he asked.

The wise fool nodded eagerly. As he did so, the judge tugged away the cloth.

There was nothing underneath.

Or, at least, nothing visible.

Fearing he was about to be the brunt of a joke, the judge demanded to be told what was going on.

'Please believe me,' Nasrudin said firmly. 'The microscope is there in front of you, but it's just so small that it can't be seen with a naked eye. Indeed, it's so tiny that you need a special microscope with which to see it.'

'And where can we find such a microscope, with which to see your microscope?'

Nasrudin huffed.

'It's right there beside the even smaller microscope,' he said impatiently.

'Where?'

'There.'

'I can't see it!' the judge barked.

'Of course you can't. You see, it's so small that you'll need to view it through the even more special microscope to its left!'

KANDAHAR
AFGHANISTAN

The Learning Process

 o one paid Nasrudin any attention.
Most of the time he was content to be an invisible pawn in society. But, once in a while, he craved attention.

And it was for that reason he started travelling.

One day, having reached Kandahar, he felt the desperate need to be appreciated. So, having spread the word, he announced that at noon next day, he would be juggling tortoises outside the tomb of King Ahmad Shah Durrani.

At the appointed time, a crowd arrived, all of them hoping to catch sight of the wise fool juggling tortoises.

A great many people had come to protest at the unnecessary cruelty to innocent creatures. But as soon as they saw that the juggling was with fluorescent green plastic tortoises, their ire abated.

At the end of the performance, everyone applauded and went on their way.

Everyone, that is, except for a haggard old man who was waiting for his daughter to collect him.

'Wise to use plastic tortoises,' he said, 'because the crowd would not have liked it if you were to juggle live animals.'

Nasrudin swallowed.

'Well, I was going to use real tortoises,' he explained, 'but, despite starting with an enormous box filled with them, none of them survived the process of learning to be juggled.'

MANHATTAN
NEW YORK

Nasrudin Rules OK

In his life as an underground radical, Nasrudin took to spraying graffiti over the city's public buildings in the dead of night.

None of the group of which he was a part were ever caught, unlike the wise fool, who was tracked, arrested, and charged.

Just before he was sentenced, the judge asked if he had anything to say.

Nasrudin nodded.

'I'd just like to ask, Your Honour, how you managed to track me down?'

The judge rolled his eyes.

'Because, unlike your associates, you signed your graffiti, and put your phone number on it as well!'

Nasrudin shrugged.

'But how else was I supposed to get the recognition I deserved?' he said.

BANGKOK
THAILAND

No Sense Sympathy

There was no food that Nasrudin liked more than spicy green curry.

While visiting Thailand, he devoured bowls of it, morning and night. Indeed, he ate so much green curry that his sense of taste was lost.

Rather than telling everyone he encountered that he loved green curry, he told them that he'd lost his sense of taste.

To his delight, people were very sympathetic. They cooed over him and pampered him in a way that he'd never been cooed over, or pampered over, before.

The day after losing his sense of taste, it returned.

Anyone else might have celebrated.

But for the wise fool, having things back to normal was a curse – a curse which ended all the cooing and the pampering.

So, pretending that he still couldn't taste, Nasrudin spread the word that he couldn't feel anything in his hands or feet, either.

The loss of a second sense guaranteed him even more sympathy than before.

The day after that, he insisted he'd gone blind. And, the day after, that he was deaf as well, *and* that he couldn't smell.

'Poor Nasrudin,' moaned one of the friends who had taken to caring for the wise fool day and night.

'I know, he can't taste, feel, smell, hear, or see,' lamented another. 'How difficult it must be to be afflicted with losing all five senses.'

The first carer looked at her friend.

'How could dear Nasrudin ever understand the mysterious ways of the senses?'

A fourth carer, who'd been silent until then, looked at the others.

'He may not understand the mysterious ways of the senses,' she exclaimed in an ice-cold voice, 'but he seems to understand the less mysterious ways of the sympathetic!'

LONDON

ENGLAND

Empty Headed

asrudin visited a Harley Street doctor specializing in unusual disorders, as he was suffering from a condition that was making his life intolerable.

When they were both seated in the surgery, the physician enquired as to the nature of his condition.

'I think cats are dogs, doctor,' the wise fool explained, 'and that dogs are cats.'

The doctor scribbled the details on his notepad. Then, he held up a photograph of a Labrador.

'What's this?'

'A cat.'

'Very good. Now, tell me what this animal is,' he said, holding up a photo of a Siamese cat.

'It's a poodle.'

'A most interesting case,' the physician muttered studiously. 'If you don't mind, I'd like to examine you further.'

In the hours that followed, Nasrudin was subjected to a full range of terribly unpleasant treatments. These included being subjected to blinding light and then freezing cold, having his head shaved, and electrodes stuck all over his scalp.

Once the tests were over, the doctor explained that the only way to treat the rare condition was to perform a long surgical procedure.

The operation was duly executed, and the doctor came to see the patient in the recovery room.

'I'm very pleased to say you'll make a full recovery,' the surgeon said comfortingly.

'Thank God for that,' Nasrudin beamed. 'If I may ask, what was the problem?'

'Well,' the physician said, 'somehow your brain had got turned the wrong way around. So we simply opened up your skull and flipped it around.'

The wise fool's eyes widened at the thought.

'But won't it affect anything else going on in my head?'

The surgeon sighed.

'In most cases it indeed would,' he said, 'but, having been through the contents of your skull, I can say with certainty there's nothing else going on in there to affect.'

NAROK
KENYA

Moonstruck

The adventures that Nasrudin had in Africa were the most extraordinary of his travelling life.

Friends would ask him why he returned time and again to the Dark Continent. Giving it great thought each time the question was posed, he responded with the same reply:

'Because of the moon, the African moon.'

His very favourite thing to do was to go out into the Rift Valley and stare up at the full moon, transfixed and in awe of its beauty.

In the small town of Narok, people were used to the eccentric stranger, who would often visit and do nothing else but stare up at the moon.

One night a passing couple overheard the wise fool declaring his undying love for the moon.

'Why don't you ever say such lovely things to me?' the wife grumbled at her husband.

'That's crazy Nasrudin,' he answered. 'Everyone knows he's unhinged, and that he's fallen in love with our friend up there in the sky.'

'He's a true romantic,' the woman sighed.

'He's a true lunatic,' her husband corrected.

ATLANTA
GEORGIA

Mysteries of Humour

Nasrudin thought of a joke which was so funny that anyone who heard it died from laughter.

As the person who'd thought of the joke in the first place, he was apparently immune to its effect. Fearful the joke would decimate society, he involved others – experts in the science of humour.

The problem was that as soon as any of the experts heard the joke, they collapsed and died like everyone else.

So, the wise fool had no choice but to carry on alone, working day and night to come up with an antidote to the joke, which was causing death on a mass scale.

After months of experimentation, he found it.

The antidote that worked against all strains of the joke now circulating was a single word yelled very loudly:

SPONGE!!!

TAHIR SHAH

Wasting no time, Nasrudin hurried to CNN's studios in Atlanta, and bellowed the antidote over and over.

'If you're alive,' he gasped, 'it means you still haven't heard the joke.'

'But how will people know the killer joke when they hear it?' the news anchor asked.

'They probably won't. You see, it strikes like a poisonous, odourless gas.'

'So, are you telling them to keep yelling "SPONGE!!!" over and over until someone tells them the joke?'

'Yes! Stop repeating "SPONGE!!!" and you're opening yourself up as a target.'

The anchor thought for a moment.

'If the joke is so perilous, surely it'll burn itself out,' she said. 'After all, if it kills everyone who knows it, it won't get passed on.'

The wise fool narrowed his eyes.

'Humour works in mysterious ways,' he said.

CARACAS
VENEZUELA

Cat-thief

All Nasrudin's greatest journeys were made with his cat.

The two had been inseparable for many years and, although quite different in character, they shared a deep affection for one another.

On a journey through Latin America, the cat was stolen.

Nasrudin and his pet had checked into a hotel in downtown Caracas. The walls of the establishment were paper thin, and the wise fool could clearly hear his cat mewling in the next room.

When he knocked on the door, a burly man opened it, glowered at him angrily, and demanded to know why he was being disturbed.

'I think my cat has somehow got into your room,' the wise fool stammered. 'I do apologize. She's terribly curious, and is always escaping me.'

'There's no cat in here,' the burly man answered, his tone threatening.

As the words were spoken, Nasrudin spotted his cat sitting on the bed.

'But… but…' he stammered

The door slammed shut.

Distraught, Nasrudin racked his brains as he wondered how to get his beloved cat back. He thought of waiting until the man went out, then getting the maid to let him into the cat-thief's room.

But the man never seemed to go anywhere.

For days, he did nothing but listen at the wall to the neighbouring room, his ear pressed up to a glass.

From what he could hear, apart from a lot of mewling and some purring, the man tended to fall into a deep, childlike sleep at three each afternoon, and only wake up once the sun had gone down.

As the hotel's air-conditioning wasn't working, the man left his window wide open.

After a week of plotting and planning, Nasrudin went out and bought supplies, then hurried back to his room.

He'd found a party shop and bought a full-body pigeon costume.

In any other circumstances he'd have felt stupid, which he most certainly was. But desperate times called for desperate measures.

So, throwing caution to the wind, he put the costume on, opened the window as wide as it would go, and crawled down the ledge to the next room.

As he'd hoped, the window was open.

Pushing the curtains open, the wise fool heard the deafening sound of snoring, and spotted his pet lying on the cat-thief's stomach.

Clambering in through the window in his disguise was far more challenging than Nasrudin had hoped, but he eventually managed to get inside the room.

On tiptoes, he made his way across the room and prepared to grab the cat with his pigeon wings.

But, as his shadow fell over the bed, the burly cat-thief woke up.

Startled and enraged at having been woken from a dream, he started throttling Nasrudin.

'How dare you break in here!' he shrieked.

'But... but... But I'm not the guy from next door as I assume you think I am,' Nasrudin choked, as his face turned bright red. 'I'm just a little pigeon who flew in through the window... *tweet, tweet, tweet!*'

The cat-thief stopped in his tracks, leaving the wise fool gasping for breath.

'Do you really expect me to believe such a preposterous story as that?!' he yelled.

'No, no, no...' Nasrudin whimpered. 'But, as you can see, I am making the most of a poor hand dealt to me by fate!'

N'DJAMENA
CHAD

Time to Decide

asrudin met the leader of Chad at a distant oasis, where he had been taken to survey the desert.

The leader declared that if there wasn't a way to put a stop to the ever-encroaching sands, starvation would ensue.

By chance, the wise fool had invented a process that caused rain to fall whenever needed. The breakthrough had occurred when he was trying to invent something else. As a result, he was rather embarrassed about it, and had kept it to himself. But, seeing the look of desperation in the president's eyes, he made an offer.

'If you provide me with a team, and a handful of supplies, I'll turn the desert into the most fertile land on the continent.'

'Is that really possible?'

'Of course,' Nasrudin retorted. 'It's far easier than it sounds.'

'How long will it take?' the president probed.

Nasrudin shrugged.

'A month or two at most.'

True to his word, the wise fool made it rain like it had never rained before.

It rained and it rained, and it rained and it rained.

Almost at once, thick green grass replaced the desert.

At first, everyone was thrilled. They applauded the stranger and his rain-making technique, and they pledged undying support to the president.

But, as time passed, people began to grumble.

They remembered out loud how beautiful the desert had looked, and how they had zigzagged their way across it.

Wishing to stay in favour, the president summoned the wise fool to the palace.

'My people are complaining.'

'Why?'

'Because they say there's too much green grass and not enough sand desert.'

'I merely did as you asked, Your Magnificence.'

'I know, but they have lived with desert for centuries, and now they miss it.'

Nasrudin's face flushed with irritation.

'When there was desert, they wanted green fields,' he remonstrated, 'but now that they have green fields, they want their desert back.'

'That is correct,' said the president.

'Why the hell can't they make up their minds?!'

RIO DE JANEIRO
BRAZIL

Nasrudin's New Clothes

asrudin arrived in Rio just in time for the annual carnival.

Everyone he met was taking part in the festivities, and it wasn't long before his friends had cajoled him to appear on one of the hundreds of carnival floats.

But, unable to speak Portuguese and not knowing his way around the shops, he couldn't get his hands on a costume.

The night before he was due to perform, a shifty-looking man called Paulo offered to make him a costume.

Nasrudin was thrilled out of his mind.

'Have you made costumes before?' he asked Paulo.

'*Sim senhor*, hundreds of costumes. Everyone comes to me when they want the very best work at the very best prices.'

'What are your prices?' Nasrudin asked.

'Three hundred American dollars.'

'That's a fortune!'

'Take it or leave it.'

'OK, I'll take it, but only because there's no other choice.'

Reluctantly, the wise fool parted with all his money.

'So, what costume do you want, *senhor*?'

Nasrudin thought for a moment.

'I'd like to go as a tiger! Can you make me the very best tiger costume that Rio's ever seen?'

Paulo nodded.

'Will you work all night?'

Again, Paulo nodded.

'Shall I meet you here tomorrow morning at nine?'

'OK.'

'Promise you won't let me down?'

Paulo the designer gave a thumbs up and grinned.

Next morning, Nasrudin went to the street corner and waited for Paulo.

But he didn't turn up.

The wise fool was furious, but he didn't have Paulo's contact details – and even if he had, it wouldn't have made any difference.

That afternoon, the carnival float on which Nasrudin had been booked to perform arrived at the designated muster point.

Nasrudin climbed up onto the float, took off all his clothes, and unfurled a banner, which read:

'A Tale of the Fool's New Clothes.'

HAARLEM
THE NETHERLANDS

The Outcast

Nasrudin had been left-handed since birth and was a founder member of the International Left-Handed Society.

One day, during his travels in Holland to promote left-handed culture, he discovered he wasn't left-handed any longer.

Horrified, he went to see a psychiatrist, who diagnosed that the patient had lived with what was known as 'temporary left-handedness'.

'That's the worst news I could have ever expected to hear,' Nasrudin gasped.

'What do you mean?' the doctor responded. 'After all, the world is very much arranged for right-handed people.'

'But, doctor, you don't understand… I am the President of the Left-Handed Society! And, as such, the one quality I must have to keep my position is to be left-handed!'

The physician agreed that the reversal was unfortunate.

'Can't you find a way to make me just a little left-handed in the middle of the week?' the wise fool asked. 'That way, I'd have the best of both worlds.'

The psychiatrist dismissed the very thought as preposterous.

'Again, I urge you to embrace being the same as most of the population – all of us right-handed people.'

Nasrudin sighed.

'Being left-handed gave me a sense of belonging,' he moaned. 'Now that I'm no longer left-handed, I'm an outcast.'

TUAMOTU
POLYNESIA

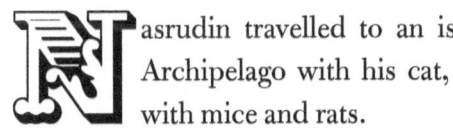

Queen Cat

asrudin travelled to an island in the Tuamotu Archipelago with his cat, and found it infested with mice and rats.

There were so many rodents that the people living there lived in limbo between hell and paradise.

The wise fool had planned to set himself up in business as a barber. But, as soon as he had seen the rodent scourge for himself, he let his pet cat free. In one bound, the animal began to slaughter every rat and mouse in sight.

Within a week, every last rodent had been hunted and devoured. The cat, now overweight, sat in the shade, purring with satisfaction. Having done well for himself as a barber, the animal's owner lay nearby in a hammock. Better still, he'd received much adulation from the locals for bringing a pet cat with him on his travels.

Once the rodents were gone, the people of the island erected an altar dedicated to their feline saviour. And, around it, they built a shrine. When the structure was complete, they sculpted little effigies from driftwood and put them outside their homes.

One morning, every last man, woman and child trooped to the hammock where the wise fool was lying. Opening an eye, the visitor expected to be lavished with yet more praise.

But the islanders did not laud him.

Rather, they had come to worship the cat.

'I think I ought to remind you,' Nasrudin said, sitting upright, 'that, as the person who brought the rodent-devourer to your island, I should be getting some of the praise.'

The tribal leader spoke for all the rest:

'From this moment,' he intoned, 'the cat will be called "Tutumaku", and she will be our queen.'

'But she's my cat,' the wise fool replied.

'No, she is not,' the elder responded. 'She's not your cat. She doesn't belong to you or anyone else.'

Nasrudin flinched.

'Shall we ask her whether she wants to be your queen or continue to be *my* cat?'

'Very well,' the chief of the islanders spoke.

So the cat was taken to a clearing in the middle of the island, with the villagers on one side and her former owner on the other.

On their side of the clearing, the locals had placed a bowl of freshly prepared meat. Eyeing the food with delight, the cat began to stride over and feast.

'We know our beloved Queen Tutumaku!' the villagers yelled.

But Nasrudin whistled loudly.

Turning around, the rodent-slaying member of royalty spied an even larger bowl of meat on the other side of the clearing.

Nasrudin may have had no meat, but he did have the magnifying mirror he used when shaving his customers' faces. He'd simply reflected the villagers' bowl of meat, making it appear far larger than it actually was.

The cat ran over, its eyes wide.

'You may know your queen,' he exclaimed, 'but I know my cat!'

HAVANA
CUBA

Progression

Nasrudin managed to get a meeting with Fidel Castro days before the legendary revolutionary leader expired.

Billing it as what was likely to be the last interview, he sold the story in advance to the *New York Times* for a huge fee.

Although bed-bound, Castro was still energetic, his eyes still burning with their characteristic fire.

Nasrudin had never interviewed such a legendary leader before and was daunted. Rather than asking him about matters of state, he read out his first question:

'Can you please tell me, O Great President of the Republic, what brand of running shoes you use?'

Castro grunted.

'I no longer have need for running shoes, but I used to run in Cuban-made shoes!'

The wise fool read out his second question:

'O Great President of the Republic, would you tell me what you think of my shirt?'

The revolutionary leader balked.

'Your shirt? Well, it's nice enough.'

Then Nasrudin read the third question:

'And, O Great President of the Republic, what do you think of my belt?'

Again, Fidel Castro flinched.

'What kind of questions are these?!' he snapped, his patience tested. 'Have you come here to talk about important matters or not?!'

'Well,' Nasrudin answered enthusiastically, 'if it's OK with you, I thought we could start with little questions, then progress to the bigger ones once we're both warmed up.'

TABORA
TANZANIA

The Aardvark

igers, snow leopards, and hyenas have fangs, but termites possess something far more terrible – mandibles.

Day and night they gnawed in a way that Nasrudin had never imagined gnawing could feel. At the end of his tether, he sought the expert advice of an entomologist.

'There is only one way to deal with the termites,' she said darkly.

'And, pray tell, what would that be?' the wise fool said, moaning, both hands clutched to his stomach.

'An aardvark.'

And so, hardly in a fit state to travel, Nasrudin set off for the great hinterland of Tanzania. And, once calmed by the cool air sweeping across the plains, he positioned himself between a pair of great termite mounds. Then, lying on his stomach, he opened his mouth, and waited.

With so many termite mounds between one horizon and the next, and so few aardvarks to go around, it took a long while before one of the creatures turned up.

Luckily, fortune was on the wise fool's side, and the aardvark in question was exceptionally dim. Assuming the open mouth to be a burrow of some kind, as others had done before it, the creature slipped inside.

Jumping to his feet, Nasrudin punched a fist in the air.

'That'll teach you, you wretched termites!'

PARIS
FRANCE

Up is Down, Down is Up

Knowing full well that Nasrudin was terrified of heights, an acquaintance challenged him to go up the Eiffel Tower and take in the view from the top.

Having paced all night in worry, the wise fool arrived at the foot of the Parisian monument at the appointed hour.

His complexion was white as a sheet, and he was shaking so much that he could hardly walk.

But as he approached the iron structure, he had an idea.

While his challenger watched, Nasrudin strode over to one of the monument's feet. And, flipping himself upside down, he clung hold of it.

'Ah yes!' he cackled. 'A magnificent view, just as you said!'

The challenger screwed up his face.

'Don't pretend you're at the top, because you are not!'

Still clinging hold, Nasrudin rejoined:

'As our little planet spins through time and space, who is to say what is up and what is down?!'

LONDON
ENGLAND

In Stock

Nasrudin was passing the Tower of London when he spotted a sign saying that entrance to view the Crown Jewels was half price.

Thrilled at saving funds, he paid his money and went inside.

After waiting for what seemed like an eternity, he reached the end of the queue and found himself face to face with the jewels.

Overcome with a blend of enthusiasm and raw greed, he reached out and grabbed one of the diamond-encrusted tiaras.

Instantly, alarms sounded, and the wise fool was arrested for theft.

'I'm so sorry, but I thought it was covered in the price of the entrance ticket,' he said remorsefully.

'If everyone helped themselves to a tiara,' the officer who'd cuffed him barked, 'we'd soon run out of jewels!'

Nasrudin seemed surprised.

'Oh,' he said in disappointment. 'You'd such a long line of visitors I assumed you'd have plenty of stock in the back.'

NUUK

GREENLAND

Standards Slipping

Nasrudin had always wanted to visit Greenland, which he had imagined to be a paradise of verdant landscapes, stretching as far as the eye could see.

But, having arrived in Greenland's capital in mid-winter, the wise fool found it to be a frozen tundra of snow and ice.

Marching to Nuuk's tourist office, Nasrudin demanded his money back.

'I've been swindled!' he cried.

The official on duty did her best to calm the irate foreigner.

'By the spring, the snow melts,' she said in a kind voice, 'and the hillsides are a delight to behold.'

But the wise fool's ire was not assuaged.

'Your country is called GREENLAND!' he declared. 'That means it's supposed to be GREEN!'

Again, the official offered her condolences.

'I'm going to dedicate my life to warning others!' Nasrudin growled. 'Because if I don't, standards elsewhere will start slipping!'

CHICAGO
ILLINOIS

Time in a Jar

asrudin could only afford a single shoe, and so was forced to hop everywhere.

As a result, even travelling a few feet took him ages.

Spotting the wise fool hopping down the street, one of his friends called out:

'What's going through your mind, you crazy man?'

'I'm saving money by hopping because I only have one shoe.'

'But that's no way to live,' the friend replied.

Nasrudin, who was hopping about on the spot, replied:

'Perhaps not. But I don't have the luxury to operate like other people.'

'You have to ask yourself what you have an abundance of,' his friend said.

'I'm not sure that I have an abundance of anything,' he answered. 'But I know what I *don't* have – money, food, somewhere to live, or a full pair of shoes.'

'Look at yourself in a different way, and you'll see that there's at least one thing you have in abundance,' his friend urged.

So, pausing on a park bench, Nasrudin thought.

He thought and he thought.

And, suddenly, he realized his friend had been right. There was something of which he had an abundance...

Time.

With nothing else of any value at all, the wise fool swapped his single shoe for four jars of varying sizes.

Then, sticking labels to each one, he marked them as containing:

Ten minutes, thirty minutes, one hour, five hours.

Sitting on the ground, he offered the jars for sale.

It wasn't long before a customer ambled up and enquired what the jars contained.

'Time,' the wise fool responded. 'The first is the cheapest because it's got just ten minutes inside. The others have more time in them, and that's why they're not only larger, but more costly.'

No one believed that the jars contained the unusual contents advertised on the labels, but people were so amused by them that they started buying Time in a Jar.

Within a week or two, Nasrudin had a thriving business, with Time in a Jar outlets all over the United States. He'd made so much cash that he had repaid all his debts, bought an apartment, a huge stock of jars, and a pair of expensive running shoes.

Nasrudin became something of a celebrity, and was invited on a leading talk show. Walking on in his new sneakers, he was holding a couple of jars filled with time.

The host asked whether he actually believed whether there was time in the jars.

'I'm willing to believe anything,' said Nasrudin, 'if it means I can walk on two feet!'

AINTREE
ENGLAND

One Man's Loss

asrudin turned up at Aintree right in time for the Grand National.

But, from the moment of his arrival, hoots of laughter erupted wherever he went. All the other animals entered for the prestigious race were thoroughbred horses, and he had turned up with his donkey.

When it came his turn to register, everyone assumed it was some kind of practical joke.

But Nasrudin wasn't joking.

'We don't allow donkeys in the Grand National,' the chief officials declared pointedly.

'Show me the rule that says a donkey can't be entered.'

The rule-book was brought out and dusted off.

Despite thumbing through it with great care, none of the officials could find a rule that prohibited donkeys from entering.

After a great deal of ill-feeling on the part of the officials, the donkey was given a number, and Nasrudin was informed he could ride – so long as he and his animal caused no trouble to anyone else.

Mounting his steed, the wise fool directed the creature to the starting box.

The starting gun sounded, and the box's door flew back.

While the other animals charged ahead full-tilt, the donkey sauntered slowly from the starting box and walked about chewing pasture, Nasrudin on her back.

The donkey grazed for a good long while. And, when the race was at an end, the wise fool was treated to a slap-up tea, and even got to meet members of the royal family.

Just as he was about to ride his donkey off into the sunset, a journalist asked Nasrudin whether he'd felt terribly humiliated by losing.

'Humiliated?' he asked. 'On the contrary, we didn't lose. We won!'

'But you didn't even finish the course!' the journalist said.

'My friend,' Nasrudin retorted, 'my donkey has eaten her fill of the most succulent grass imaginable, while I have had a reason to get all dressed up, and have had a fine day out. You may think that's losing... but the way I see it, one man's loss is another man's good fortune.'

MOSCOW
RUSSIA

The Map

While working as a hacker at an illegal troll factory, the wise fool was lured to an address at the edge of the city and was arrested by agents of the Federal Security Service.

'We know you hacked into the government mainframe!' the commander yelled, as the suspect's hands were cuffed behind his back. 'If you tell us how you performed the hack we are likely to be more lenient with you.'

Nasrudin, who wasn't relishing the thought of spending the next twenty years in a cell at the infamous Vladimir Central Prison, promised to cooperate.

Having been led into an interrogation chamber, replete with torture equipment, he was given a paper and pencil.

'Draw me a route map!' the commander barked.

Swallowing hard, Nasrudin did his best to remember.

Fifteen minutes later, he slid the paper back across the table.

The commander scrutinized an incredibly complex diagram and smiled to himself. The fact that the suspect was cooperating so well, and providing what looked like first-rate information, meant he would be up for promotion.

'Is this the precise route you took through cyberspace?' he growled.

Balking at the question, Nasrudin shook his head left, right, left.

'Then, what is it?'

'It's the route the taxi took to get me here,' he replied, wide-eyed. 'The traffic was terrible!'

LAPLAND
SWEDEN

Humiliation for the Heavens

asrudin had spent his entire savings to get from his village to the very top of Lapland, in order to view the legendary Northern Lights.

Although the wise fool wasn't especially interested in witnessing the natural phenomenon, the head of his village had seen them, and never stopped going on about it.

So, in a bid to get even, he made the journey.

Having wrapped up in many layers of woollen clothing, he went outside and stared up at the sky.

The clouds moved, and the spectacular phosphorescent light show shone down.

'Well, that's not very impressive!' Nasrudin yelled up at the heavens. 'Surely you can do better than that!'

A local man exited the lodge at which the foreigner was staying and overheard the insults being directed at the sky.

'The Northern Lights are the most awesome display of nature,' he said.

Nasrudin shook his head.

'No they're not!' he boomed. 'They're lousy! If I were the sky up there I'd be embarrassed! You're second-rate Northern Lights!'

The local appeared saddened.

Feeling a pang of guilt, the wise fool cupped his mouth to the local man's ear.

'I'm only jeering at the sky to humiliate it,' he whispered, 'so it gives me the very best display possible.'

BRATISLAVA
SLOVAKIA

Bird Talk

asrudin had been in Bratislava for months, taking a course on basket-weaving.

One night, he dreamt he was a little red-breasted robin.

When he woke up, he was amazed to find he couldn't speak, but could only tweet like a robin.

He was wondering what to do, when there was a thump at the door.

Nasrudin opened it, to find an immigration official standing in the frame.

'Are you Nasrudin?'

'Tweet tweet.'

'You've overstayed your visa, and so I've come to arrest you!'

'Tweet tweet!'

'Are you trying to make fun of me?'

'Tweet tweet!'

'Show me your passport!'

'Tweet tweet!'

The official got out his handcuffs.

'Can't you see I've turned into a bird?!' Nasrudin cried out, as his wrists were cuffed together behind his back. 'I can't understand anything you're saying!'

MOUNTAIN VIEW
CALIFORNIA

The Lying Inventor

Fascinated by the concept of social media, Nasrudin tried his best to get noticed as a pioneer, even though he had no skills or training.

Through pestering other peoples' contacts, he was invited to an interview at Google's Advanced Technology and Projects.

'Well, Mr. Nasrudin,' the head of the department said, 'I hear that you've invented something we may be interested in here at Google.'

The wise fool nodded enthusiastically.

'Yes, I've invented a machine to capture peoples' dreams,' he replied. 'So that the dreams, along with all the dreamer's personal data, can be uploaded by Bluetooth from the dreamer's brain to a server online.'

The head of the department swallowed hard.

'That sounds remarkable,' she said. 'How did you ever come up with such a machine?'

Nasrudin sniffed casually.

'Oh, I just thought of it, and before I knew it, I'd created it.'

'That sounds as though you have an extraordinary gift. Tell me… have you invented other things before?'

'Gosh, yes, lots of things.'

'Can you give me some examples?'

The wise fool rubbed a hand over his cheek, and answered:

'Soap, dogs, perfume, apples, and all kinds of other stuff.'

'But those are all things which have existed for centuries.'

'Really?'

'Yes.'

'Then,' Nasrudin replied, 'you may be wise not to believe a word I say.'

ETOSHA
NAMIBIA

The Tracker

In his role as a naturalist, Nasrudin had come to be known as an expert tracker.

No matter where he ventured, he could track all manner of animals – at least that was the reputation he made for himself.

On one occasion, the wise fool was on an expedition through Etosha, the great Namibian game reserve. Day after day, he went out long before dawn and tracked animals, showing his discoveries to the others in the group later in the day.

A local game warden, who was in charge of the expedition, had disliked the wise fool right from the start and could see through his claims. Indeed, anyone who'd spent more than five minutes in the bush could see he was a phoney.

But, fortunately for the wise fool, no one else in the expedition had ever been to Africa before.

During a full week of game rides, Nasrudin pointed out all kinds of tracks, some of them very rare indeed. Each day the tracks he discovered were more exceptional than the day before, and Nasrudin himself was more enthusiastic.

A point came at which the game warden couldn't stand it any longer.

'Are you questioning Nasrudin's skill as a tracker?' a member of the group called out.

'Yes, I am! He has no skill and is a complete fraud!'

The wise fool's back warmed with anger.

'That's not true!' he riposted. 'I've tracked animals in deserts all over the world.'

The warden jabbed a hand down at the ground, at a track that the expert claimed to have just located.

'From what I can see,' he said, studying the tracks, 'it has three feet – each of varying sizes – a wheel, and a ten-foot tail that drags along behind it.'

'Yes!' Nasrudin bellowed. 'How exciting I happened upon it!'

The warden grimaced.

'Believe me, there's no animal out here with three feet, a wheel, and a long dragging tail.'

The team looked at the tracker.

'Don't blame me.'

'Then who should we blame?' the warden asked.

'My enthusiasm!' bawled Nasrudin.

MEXICO CITY
MEXICO

No Truth

After being based in Mexico for several months, Nasrudin got hooked on the leading soap opera, *Rosa Salvaje – Savage Rose*.

Each time an episode was broadcast, he was glued to the screen, hanging on every word.

Naturally, being the wise fool, he believed it all.

One day, by chance, he happened to see Rosa, the lead character from the show, crossing the street in Mexico City.

Sprinting down the street, he caught up with her.

'I love you!' he swooned. 'You're so wonderful!'

The actress who played Rosa was used to being stopped in the street.

Giving thanks, she strode on.

But Nasrudin pursued her.

'Listen, mister,' she said icily, 'you have to understand I'm just an actress, and I am not really Rosa.'

'Hush!' Nasrudin cried in horror. 'How ever could you say such a thing?'

He thought for a moment, and added:

'Ah, but of course, the real Rosa would pretend to be an actress, such is her modesty!'

The actress changed tack.

'All right! I *am* Rosa!'

'Hah! I knew it!'

Spying a potential public disturbance, a police officer stepped out of the shadows.

As he did so, the actress attacked Nasrudin:

'OK! I am NOT Rosa!' she screamed at the top of her lungs. 'And that's the truth!'

The officer grabbed the fan by the arm.

'I'm warning you… if you don't go on your way, I'll arrest you! This actress had told you the truth – that she is *not* Rosa Salvaje!'

'My dear officer!' Nasrudin responded. 'Who are you to decide whether I can handle the truth?!'

CAPE CANAVERAL
FLORIDA

Moon Lizards

asrudin was chosen to go into space for NASA, having been selected after claiming fraudulently that he'd been up on the moon loads of times.

The night before the take-off, the wise fool was seen crawling around the launch pad on his hands and knees.

'What are you doing, Nasrudin?' a technician asked.

'I'm just checking.'

'Checking for what?'

'Checking for moon lizards.'

'Whatever for?'

Nasrudin regarded the technician incredulously.

'Everyone knows that if there are no moon lizards, the mission will have to be called off!'

'Remind me – which space agency were you with before NASA?'

'It was called Daydream-45.'

KOLKATA
INDIA

Suspended Disbelief

Since early childhood, Nasrudin had been terrified of ghost stories.

As a teenager, the fear continued on to horror movies, which he avoided like the plague. The mere mention of them sent him into convulsions.

During time spent in India, studying the illusions used by so-called 'godmen', the wise fool attracted the advances of a Bengali woman. Unlike him, she adored the most chilling horror movies, and liked nothing more than describing the plots of her favourite films.

One afternoon, while perusing the used bookstalls on College Street, Nasrudin happened to see the horror-obsessed woman out of the corner of his eye.

She was moving fast in his direction.

Thinking on his feet, he fumbled for his mobile phone, so that he could pretend to be talking to a friend. But he'd left it in the hotel. Unfazed, he took off his left shoe and held it to his ear.

'Thank you so much for the invitation,' he said, speaking into the shoe, 'it would be an honour for me to accept.'

The Bengali woman tapped him on the shoulder.

'D'you realize that you're talking into your shoe?'

The wise fool pretended to hang up the call.

Turning to the woman, he said:

'Tell me… you love horror movies, do you not?'

'Yes.'

'And in those movies gruesome things happen which you know in reality are merely acting?'

'Of course they are. D'you really think all the death and gore is done for real?'

'Well, in talking to my friend a moment ago,' Nasrudin said, 'I was simply relying on the same system of pretend as is used in the movies you so adore. So, if it's not too much, I ask that you pretend you're at the cinema, and suspend disbelief.'

CAMBRIDGE
ENGLAND

Testing, Testing

During post-graduate studies at Cambridge University, Nasrudin involved himself with the physics of force.

Never one to shy away from practical experiment, he paid a circus troupe to fire him out of a cannon.

Although donning a crash helmet, he had forgotten to wear boots. As a result, his feet were badly burned.

Taken to hospital by ambulance, the wise fool found himself explaining what had happened.

'I was simply testing the laws of physics,' he explained.

'But what new data could you have hoped to gather?' the surgeon asked. 'After all, people have studied such things for centuries.'

'That may well be true,' Nasrudin said, glancing down at his bandaged feet. 'But who is to say the laws of physics don't change once in a while?'

HUDSON
NEW YORK

Wrong Experience

Nasrudin got a job as a busboy in a diner upstate.

From day one he proved to be the worst person who'd ever held the job.

Horrified, the owner of the establishment reprimanded him for spilling soup over one regular's lap, slipping and accidentally stabbing another with a steak knife, and causing a riot in the kitchen.

'How dare you claim to have experience!' the owner barked, his face flushed with rage.

'But I do have experience,' Nasrudin retorted haughtily. 'Just not in doing what you're asking me to do.'

WASHINGTON DC

Second-rate Untruth

On a visit to the capital, Nasrudin went on a tour of the White House.

Unable to keep to the specified route, he ambled off alone, and after numerous wrong turns, found himself in the Oval Office.

Without any fear at all, he went over to the presidential partners' desk and sat down behind it.

Just as he was getting comfortable, a secret service agent burst in and arrested the wise fool.

That afternoon, he appeared before a judge – the courtroom packed to capacity with journalists, all of them intrigued to know what the intruder had been thinking.

When the court was in session, the judge asked the accused why he'd sat on the president's chair.

'You misunderstand,' Nasrudin answered. 'I wasn't sitting at the desk.'

'Yes you were!' the judge shouted. 'We have CCTV footage to prove it.'

'Ah, but you're mistaken. You see, I wasn't there in the capacity of a person, so much as in the capacity of a cushion.'

Sensing insubordination, the judge clenched his fists.

'What?!'

'As I say, I sat on the chair not as a member of the public, but rather as a cushion for the president's behind,' Nasrudin explained.

The judge was furious.

'D'you really expect me to believe that?!'

'No,' the wise fool responded, 'but in this case my gut's telling me that a second-rate untruth is better than a first-rate truth.'

LETICIA
COLOMBIA

The Black Panther

Indigestion from an aardvark is, as it so happens, exceptionally horrid.

So horrid, that Nasrudin was almost unable to walk, talk, or do anything else. Moaning, groaning, and feeling terrible pity for himself, he phoned his great aunt, because she always had good advice to give.

'You stupid boy for swallowing an aardvark!' she scolded. 'Everyone knows swallowing aardvarks leads to nothing but trouble! Don't expect that you'll ever find a wife, behaving like that!'

'But, I'm not trying to find a wife, Auntie.'

'Of course you are!' the great aunt shot back. 'Every young man – whether they have an aardvark inside them or not – should be thinking of nothing but matrimony!'

'What should I do, Auntie?' Nasrudin groaned.

'Go on one of those match-making sites on the internet… that's what all good young boys your age are doing.'

'No… not to find a wife, but to deal with the aardvark in my stomach.'

The wise fool's great aunt sighed long and hard.

'You'd better swallow a black panther,' she said knowingly. 'Because black panthers gobble up aardvarks in three seconds flat.'

'But where would I find a black panther, Auntie?'

Again, the old woman sighed down the phone.

'In Colombia, of course,' she said.

So, following orders, Nasrudin made a beeline for the Colombian jungle, his stomach in turmoil like it had never been before.

Three days after arriving, he was borne on a stretcher into the jungle by members of the Witoto tribe, and was laid on the ground. Unable to flip over onto his stomach, the wise fool closed his eyes and opened his mouth.

The afternoon melted into dusk, and dusk into night.

Nasrudin waited.

Eventually, a black panther prowled from the undergrowth, curious at why intruders had trespassed on its territory.

Seeing a human lying outstretched, mouth open and eyes closed, the panther prepared to strike. Fangs and claws glinting in the moonlight, the panther leapt at the prey.

Although in a pitiful state, Nasrudin managed to thwart the attack and, in a movement of impressive finesse, swallowed the pouncing panther whole.

His spirits rejuvenated, he jumped up and punched a hand in the air.

'Don't forget you're looking for an aardvark, you damned panther!' he cried.

MANHATTAN
NEW YORK

The Drowning Man

Nasrudin had tricked his way into a leading advertising firm on Madison Avenue.

Over a period of months, he developed a string of campaigns – selling everything from soap powder to jet aircraft.

In the history of advertising, no one had ever had such a run of extraordinary good fortune. As a result, the wise fool was feted wherever he went, with the fraternity of ad-men eager to know the secret of his success.

In an interview with *Vanity Fair*, he decided to reveal the way he'd got to the top in the blink of an eye.

'All I do is to imagine I'm a mouse drowning in a bowl of water.'

The reporter flinched.

'Don't get you, Mr. Nasrudin.'

'Well, it's simplicity itself... I set my mind to the campaign at hand, and imagine I'll sink deep under the surface if I don't come up with the goods.'

'But surely that doesn't explain your astonishing success?'

The wise fool slipped the journalist a sideways glance.

'Never underestimate the ability of a drowning man,' he said.

MIAMI
FLORIDA

Teaching by Example

While visiting Florida, Nasrudin stayed with his sister and her teenaged son.

'Having you here will do a world of good for little Adam,' his sister said. 'You see, as his father's away most of the time, he doesn't have a role model.'

Proud at being thought of as a positive example, the wise fool promised to be the best role model in the history of role models.

Next morning, he took little Adam to a grocery shop.

'Now, I want you to watch what I do and say,' he said. 'Because I'm going to demonstrate how not to behave. Do you understand?'

His nephew gave a thumbs up.

Nasrudin grabbed a frozen chicken from one of the freezers and stuffed it down his shirt. Then, he filled his pockets with sweets.

Watching on CCTV, the manager hurried over and ordered the wise fool to put the things back.

'I'm just teaching my nephew here how not to behave,' he said with a smile.

'I don't care what you're doing,' the manager reposted. 'You've got to put those things back at once or I'll call the cops.'

'Call them, you damned fool!' Nasrudin barked.

Within a minute or two, the police arrived and slapped Adam's uncle in handcuffs.

'You deserve a good kicking!' Nasrudin barked at the officer as he was taken away.

Next day, he appeared in court, where he was rebuked for his shocking behaviour.

Spotting his sister and nephew in the court, he raised his hands above his head and shouted at the judge:

'If you were any more ugly, you could get work in a freak show!'

A long sentence was given, and Nasrudin was sent to jail – where he was beaten, humiliated, and locked in a cell with a convicted murderer.

After many months, he was freed, his face and body raw with wounds.

Making his way back to his sister's home, he found Adam getting ready to go to bed.

'I hope you understood the lessons I have taught you,' he uttered earnestly. 'If you steal, and yell at officials, what happens to you is what I got.'

The boy's mother shuffled in from the kitchen and looked at her beloved brother as though he was insane.

'Why didn't you simply tell Adam how not to behave and leave it at that?' she moaned.

The wise fool smiled obliquely.

'Because it's always best to explain through example,' he said.

SACRAMENTO
CALIFORNIA

Late Again

asrudin was reading an old book to his son one evening that described a fantastic gold rush at the Sacramento River.

All night, he dreamed of the thrill of digging the yellow metal from the ground and panning it in the river.

Next day, unable to control himself, the wise fool packed his bags, kissed his little son farewell, and set off to make his fame and fortune in the gold rush.

Having made a zigzag journey from Central Asia to northern California, Nasrudin reached the brow of a hill. According to his son's book, beyond it lay the legendary gold fields.

His heart pounding like never before, and weighed down with equipment, the wise fool took in the panoramic view.

Alas, it was not one of men like he panning the silt, but rather of a modern city bustling with morning commuters.

'Hold on! Hold on!' Nasrudin yelled. 'Spare a thought for a late arrival! You all got a head start, so take a break until I catch up!'

MANHATTAN
NEW YORK

Sandcastle Trading

Blagging his way into a major investment bank, Nasrudin found himself working on Wall Street. Unlike all the other traders, he had no previous business experience. The only thing he'd ever done involving any money at all had been renting out deck chairs one summer on the beach.

But with the economy riding high, Wall Street needed all the traders it could find and, as a result, the wise fool was given a computer terminal of his own.

As soon as trading opened, he started selling shares at a massive loss.

Within a minute or two, alarm bells were sounding through the building. But the damage had already been done.

Nasrudin had lost more money than any other rogue trader in history.

Before he was escorted from the building, another trader asked what on earth he was thinking.

'Well,' he answered brightly, 'in my head I was building a sandcastle at the beach. It'd collapsed, and I was left with a hole… so I kept digging down, making the hole bigger and bigger.'

'You mean doubling down, hoping to trade your way out?'

'Yes, just like that.'

'What was the ultimate objective?'

'Well,' Nasrudin said, 'I knew that if I could scoop away all the sand in the world then I'd be able to start level with everyone else.'

MIAMI
FLORIDA

Mr. Loo Brush

No one in the United States could pronounce his name correctly, so Nasrudin registered himself as a symbol.

The symbol resembled what looked like an outline of a toilet brush.

As a result, he was the butt of a thousand jokes.

'Are you going to change your name back to Nasrudin, Mr. Loo Brush?' a wag asked.

'No, I'm not.'

'But it must be terrible to be subjected to such abuse.'

'Not at all.'

'You're enjoying being called Mr. Loo Brush?'

'Yes.'

'Why's that?'

'Well, while the shape of my name may be the butt of a great many jokes, it's never mispronounced.'

MANHATTAN
NEW YORK

Solution Booth

In his usual need for funds with which to continue his travels, Nasrudin had the idea of building an advice booth and charging passers-by for his wisdom.

Choosing a good, sunny stretch of Broadway, he took his place and waited for the first customer.

It wasn't long before someone sidled up, paid the five-dollar fee, and spewed out his life story.

'That's a terrible situation you find yourself in,' said the wise fool, having listened intently to the tale of tribulation and woe.

'That's why I've come to you and paid my money,' said the unfortunate. 'So, tell me what I should do to sort my life out.'

Nasrudin looked him in the eye and explained the solution:

'Go buy three planks of wood, a saw, some nails, paint, and a brush. Then make a booth.'

'You mean like this one?'

'Yes, exactly like this one.'

'Then what?'

'Paint a sign on the front – "Life Advice $5".'

'You mean like you've done?'

'Yes, just like I've done.'

'Then where should I put it?'

'Anywhere where there are lots of passers-by would do,' the wise fool said. 'Somewhere like right there, next to my booth.'

'What do I do then?'

'You give advice to people who come and pay a fee.'

'You mean like you do?'

'Yes. That's right.'

'But won't that put you out of business?'

'No problem about that,' Nasrudin answered. 'I promise to be your first customer.'

'Why?'

'Because I'm dying for some reliable life advice, so I can find a way out of the terrible situation I'm in!'

NAMPO
NORTH KOREA

The Reason for Braying

urious what it would be like to live as a four-legged animal, Nasrudin tracked down a surgeon in North Korea who agreed to swap his brain with that of his donkey.

Before the complex operation took place, the wise fool made the donkey promise to go along with the second procedure to swap the brains back.

From what he could understand, the donkey agreed, so the brains were swapped over.

Experiencing the world as his donkey did, Nasrudin was initially fascinated. But he quickly grew bored with the terrible food, the lack of stimulation, and with being the butt of everyone's jokes.

Meanwhile, with their brains swapped over, donkey-brain Nasrudin got on the Nasrudin-brain donkey and rode down to the river.

Dismounting, the donkey-brain Nasrudin got on his hands and knees and grazed on the long, succulent grass all afternoon.

At the end of the day, Nasrudin brayed for the donkey living in his body to have them both swapped round again.

But the donkey-brained Nasrudin didn't understand.

'Damn that bloody creature!' Nasrudin brayed from the donkey's body. 'If I could, I'd whip you within an inch of your life!'

Reduced to being a beast of burden, he moaned at his state of affairs.

'Now I understand why donkeys bray all night,' he thought. 'They've had their brains swapped with their masters, and there's no hope of ever getting them swapped back again!'

KYOTO
JAPAN

Nasrudin Extravaganza

While travelling in Japan, Nasrudin spent several weeks staying at a rented apartment in Kyoto, where he was fortunate enough to meet a well-respected scholar.

Time passed, and the two men developed a friendship, through which the wise fool learned a great deal about Japanese culture.

One day, the scholar invited his new friend for dinner at his home. Realizing it to be an honour, Nasrudin accepted readily, and looked forward to the meal and the traditional hospitality that would surely accompany it.

Arriving exactly on time, the visitor was paid compliments, thanked repeatedly for coming, and was then invited to eat in the *tatami* room, reserved for respected guests.

'I have prepared a very special dish for you,' the scholar explained.

'Does it have a name?'

'*Ikizukuri*.'

'I have not heard of that before,' Nasrudin said.

The scholar brought a large fish in from the kitchen and placed it on the floor, where a tablecloth had been laid.

Although clearly still alive, the fish had been filleted. As it hovered between life and death, the scholar cut slices, serving them raw to the honoured guest.

At the end of the evening, Nasrudin returned to his apartment. All he could think of was the live fish, as he wondered what his host had been thinking.

A few days passed.

Then, realizing he ought to reciprocate and invite the scholar to his modest apartment, Nasrudin sent an invitation, which was gratefully received.

The next evening, the scholar arrived and was greeted with a wave of praise by his host.

'I do hope you enjoy the meal I have prepared,' the wise fool crooned.

With that, he slipped into the kitchen.

A moment or two of silence passed, then Nasrudin carried a large platter through into the dining room.

In the centre of the dish was a man's shoe. It had been filled with tomato sauce, then baked. Around the edges were a dozen live frogs. And between the frogs and the shoe was a sea of lumpy custard.

Although horrified, the scholar feigned delight, then did his best to eat a little of the revolting dish.

At the end of the meal, unable to think of anything else to say, he asked if the feast had a name.

'Oh, yes!' the wise fool exclaimed boisterously. 'It's called Nasrudin Extravaganza!'

'Is it a typical dish from your country?' the scholar probed.

Nasrudin shook his head.

'We don't eat this food in my country,' he replied.

'Then, could you tell me where the Nasrudin Extravaganza comes from?'

'Nowhere,' Nasrudin answered. 'I invented it myself.'

'Very creative,' the guest whispered in horror.

An awkward silence descended.

Breaking it, the wise fool said:

'Having experienced the intriguing meal at your home, I wondered how I could match your originality… so I prepared the Nasrudin Extravaganza by rooting through the furthest limits of my imagination.'

FORT ST. JOHN
CANADA

Jump Talk

A thrill-seeker at heart, Nasrudin had seen a documentary about an elite group of smoke jumpers, who protected Canada's vast forests from wildfires.

As soon as the documentary was over, the wise fool scoured the internet until he found an application page for parachutists to train as smoke jumpers.

Needless to say, a background in parachuting and fire-fighting was expected.

Nasrudin had neither, but he did have a mountain of something else – enthusiasm.

At the interview he was grilled by a veteran of the fire service.

'So, tell me, how many jumps have you done?'

Nasrudin caught a flash of himself skipping in the gym.

'Oh hundreds… Even thousands.'

'Hundreds *or* thousands?'

'Hundreds *of* thousands!'

The interviewer appeared to be impressed.

'Really?'

The wise fool gloated at having apparently said the right thing.

'Yes. Hundreds of thousands of jumps.'

'What altitude do you usually jump from?'

'Altitude? Well, altitude doesn't really come into it.'

The interviewer frowned.

'What equipment did you make your jumps with?'

Again, Nasrudin caught a flash of himself skipping at the gym, the rope swishing up and down.

'The usual kind of gear.'

'Can you be more specific?'

'I'm not quite sure of the make or model,' he answered, 'but when it got going it moved at the speed of light.'

PULASKI
TENNESSEE

Mirror, Mirror

During his time in the United States, Nasrudin found himself glued to a TV shopping channel that touted second-rate goods.

Even though he knew full well the merchandise was second-rate, he couldn't help but be sucked in.

One day, he bought a special bathroom mirror which claimed to be designed for people with low self-esteem.

Going through a patch of depression, he bought one.

When it finally arrived, he put in the batteries, hung it on the wall, and stared into the glass.

To his absolute delight, the magic mirror showed him looking so much younger – as he had looked at least twenty years before.

During the dark days of Covid lockdown, when he was forced to do interminable Zoom calls, the wise fool positioned the magic mirror at an angle to the screen, so that people on the call would see his youthful reflection.

All was well, and Nasrudin went from strength to strength, his self-confidence boosted no end by the mirror.

But then, one morning, having clambered out of bed, he peered into the glass and was greeted with the most terrible sight.

Gone was the youthful reflection he had come to know and adore… replaced by a hideous, aged representation of himself.

Gasping and wheezing, he phoned the firm that had made the magic mirror.

'We get a lot of calls like yours,' said a calm voice on the other end.

'Your damned mirror has caused me misery like you cannot believe!' the wise fool exclaimed.

'Have no fear, sir,' said a silky voice. 'The solution is simple.'

'What is it?'

'Replace the batteries, and you'll be back to your old self.'

PYONGYANG
NORTH KOREA

Cloned Ego

Nasrudin had read a report on a site from the dark web, stating that somewhere in North Korea a rogue geneticist was making human clones for a price.

Unable to contain his excitement, the wise fool made his way to the secret state, crossed the border illegally, and spent weeks searching out the underground bunker where the geneticist was doing his work.

After much difficulty, he was admitted, and found himself face to face with the scientist.

'I want fifty clones of myself,' Nasrudin explained. 'And I'm willing to pay for every last one.'

The scientist raised an eyebrow.

'Fifty clones won't be cheap.'

'I have money, but I expect a bulk discount,' said Nasrudin.

A deal was reached and, a few weeks later, the scientist delivered the fifty clones to the wise fool's hotel.

Each one looked like him, talked like him, and was dressed like him, too.

Best of all, though, they thought like him.

Delighted, Nasrudin shepherded the clones back over the border to South Korea. Little by little, they travelled by land and sea back to Central Asia.

The wise fool found that, just as had been promised, the clones thought exactly like he did. A drawback was having to feed fifty mouths in addition to his own. And, just like him, the clones had a taste for the finer things in life but had no way to pay for them.

One morning, when he and the clones had reached home, Nasrudin gathered them around.

'Now, I am sure you have been wondering why I had myself cloned so many times,' he said.

The clones didn't answer. Instead, they stared at their master adoringly.

'I've had you all made,' the wise fool explained, 'for one reason, and one reason alone… REVENGE!'

Pulling out a dossier from a drawer, he explained how the clones would undertake missions on his behalf.

In the days that followed, the clones were dispatched.

One was ordered to go and humiliate a particular minister in the government.

Another was sent to attack a bank that had refused the wise fool an account.

Half a dozen more were instructed to retaliate against men that, as boys, had made Nasrudin's life a living hell.

Once all fifty clones had been dispatched, their master sat back and waited.

A day passed.

Then another.

And, just as Nasrudin was turning off his bedroom light, the police broke down the door.

The wise fool was captured and thrown into an interrogation cell.

'I'm innocent! I'm innocent!' he squealed.

'Innocent of what?'

'Innocent of all the crimes that people who look like me have been committing!'

Striding from the shadows, the chief torturer reached the spot where the wise fool was chained to the wall.

'We have fifty copies of you,' he said with loathing. 'Each one of them insisting they're innocent. The only question is, which one is the real Nasrudin?'

'Me! Me! Me!' yelped the prisoner.

'That's what all the others have said, too.'

'Of course it is,' Nasrudin moaned. 'Because they all think like me.'

The interrogator glared at the prisoner, wondering how best to get to the truth.

'I suppose I'll have to get on with it,' he said. 'After all, I've got fifty-one of you to torture.'

Whimpering, the wise fool began to sob.

'Surely, it's obvious that I'm the original Nasrudin,' he said, his cheeks wet with tears. 'Because who else would have been so foolish as to clone himself for the purposes of revenge?'

MARRAKECH
MOROCCO

Operation Overthink

Wherever he went in Morocco, Nasrudin saw signs for 'Chocolat des Sirènes'.

The packaging was festooned with the image of a voluptuous mermaid sitting on a slab of chocolate. There was no clear reason why the wise fool loathed the brand of confectionary as he did. All he knew was he would stop at nothing until the company that produced it had gone bankrupt.

In the weeks that followed, the wise fool bought up every bar of mermaid chocolate he could find. He ate nothing else, and certainly thought about nothing else either.

Worrying about him, a friend asked why the wise fool was trying to ruin the chocolate manufacturer by buying all its product, when it would be simpler to shun it and get others to do the same.

Nasrudin looked at his friend coldly, a sinister aspect slipping down over his face.

'The question is not whether I'm overthinking the situation,' he answered. 'But, rather, whether other people are underthinking it.'

SAN FRANCISCO
CALIFORNIA

Sharing the Grey Matter

Wherever Nasrudin went, droves of hippies were dead set on making him into a guru.

They pleaded for him to tell them to turn on, tune in, and drop out.

In response, the wise fool begged his would-be followers not to rely on him, but instead to think for themselves.

'Why should we think for ourselves, O Master,' one devotee asked, 'when you will think for us?!'

Nasrudin tapped the side of his head.

'I would if I could,' he replied. 'But, believe me, there's not enough grey matter in there for myself, let alone to share out among all of you.'

ANKARA
TURKEY

Double-bluff Humour

Nasrudin had managed to get some work as a stand-up comedian.

He'd only taken the job out of desperation and was hopeless. Despite trying, he kept mixing up the punchlines of his jokes.

Curiously, the audience found the mixed-up jokes far funnier than if they were delivered as they were supposed to be told.

Hailing the foreigner to be a comedic genius, most people assumed he was getting the punchlines wrong on purpose.

At the end of the evening, a young comedian asked Nasrudin for his secret.

'I tell terrible jokes, and I get them all mixed up,' he replied. 'It's a failsafe way to get laughs through what I call the "double-bluff".'

HOKKAIDO
JAPAN

Evolution

While studying the Way of the Ninja on the northern island of Sapporo, Nasrudin was taught that a real master crafted all his own equipment himself.

Following orders, the wise fool bought some tools and a sheet of the highest quality steel and got down to fashioning his first throwing stars. Although he had high hopes, he found it incredibly challenging to cut the metal.

The only shape he could manage to cut was a circle.

After working on his throwing stars all night, Nasrudin took the clutch of discs to the dojo, where they were examined.

'What kind of a fool are you?!' the *sensei* bellowed. They're supposed to be throwing stars!'

'That's exactly what they are, Master.'

'If they're throwing stars, why don't they have points?!'

Nasrudin bit his upper lip in worry, remembering how hard it had been to cut the steel.

'I imagine that making throwing stars is like anything else,' he responded.

'Yes, it is!'

'Excellent, Master!' Nasrudin muttered under his breath.

'And why is that excellent?!'

'Because, Master, with time I am certain evolution will show me the way.'

FLORES
INDONESIA

The Komodo Dragon

nce he had swallowed the black panther, Nasrudin spent time living with the Witoto tribe.

A noble people, the Witotos were in awe of the foreigner they came to know as 'Panther Man'. For not even in their great, epic folklore was there a character who had devoured a black panther so effortlessly.

After many days with the Witotos, the wise fool called the tribe to gather around one full-mooned night.

'I must leave you, dear friends,' he said. 'Because my stomach is not as it ought to be.'

'Are you returning to the Land of the Panthers?' a tribal elder called.

Nasrudin nodded.

'Yes, the Land of the Panthers has appeared to me in a dream, and I have been summoned.'

131

'Summoned by the Great Panther?'

Again, the wise fool dipped his head in a nod.

'Yes, the Great Panther is waiting for me.'

'How will you reach the Land of the Panthers?' a little girl at the front of the crowd asked, her face bathed in firelight.

Before the wise fool could answer, the tribal chief spoke:

'He will drink *ayahuasca*, and will see the route to the Land of Panthers!'

And so, that night, Nasrudin drank a cup of the noxious hallucinogen *ayahuasca*, and was transported to the Land of the Panthers.

In the reverie, he saw himself lying on his front on an island in a strange archipelago. As he watched, half mesmerized and half alarmed, a great lizard hurried from behind a boulder and ran full speed down his throat.

Next day, knowing what he was to do, Nasrudin bid the kind people of the Witoto tribe farewell, and he made the long and uncertain journey across the Pacific – to the island of Flores.

A day and a night after arriving, the wise fool reached the boulder he'd seen in the dream. Lying down on his front, he opened his mouth as wide as he could, and waited.

In less time than it takes to tell, a large male Komodo dragon scurried from behind the rock and into Nasrudin's mouth.

Leaping to his feet, the wise fool thrust a hand in the air and exclaimed:

'Get that damned panther, and be quick about it!'

LAU

FIJI

In Search of Proof

Nasrudin arrived on the tiny island of Lau in the Fijian archipelago.

Clambering off the boat with his donkey, he caused quite a sensation.

As cut off from the rest of the world as they were, the people of Lau had never actually touched a donkey.

Everyone was fascinated with the creature and would steal up and touch it with their hands.

Some felt its snout, others its girth, and more still its tail.

'What is it?' one of the children asked.

'It's proof,' Nasrudin replied.

'Proof of what?'

'Proof if I needed it that I've come to the right place to make a fortune!'

CHICAGO
ILLINOIS

Theory Discredited

While in Chicago, Nasrudin met a man named Lindsay Williams, who was the kindest person he'd ever encountered.

A few days later, he met a woman with the same name. She was equally as thoughtful as the male Lindsay Williams. Both were courteous, charming, intelligent, and uproariously funny.

Having pondered long and hard, the wise fool came to the conclusion that, based on the information he had accumulated, everyone called Lindsay Williams was likely to be as wonderful as the first two people he'd met with the name.

So, dropping everything, Nasrudin went online and tracked down dozens of people called Lindsay Williams. Some were in the United States, others in England, Scotland,

Australia, and New Zealand. He even found a listing for a Lindsay Williams on a remote island in Polynesia.

Once he had a definitive list of people with the name, the wise fool set about contacting them. His plan was to only have friends called Lindsay Williams from then on.

Even though it is true to say that one or two were flattered, the great majority regarded Nasrudin with suspicion.

More than a few blocked him, and some even alerted the police.

Shut out by the Lindsay Williams community, the wise fool took out his notebook. Turning to a new page, he wrote in large, red letters:

NOTE TO SELF:
LINDSAY WILLIAMS EXPOSED AS FRAUDS
THEORY DISCREDITED

MOMBASA
KENYA

Thief's Messenger

After many weeks on the road, Nasrudin's clothing was in a terrible state.

He wanted to buy something new to wear, but he couldn't spare any cash. So, while staying on the rooftop of a guesthouse, he pinched some clothes from the laundry line one night.

In the darkness, he couldn't see the pattern, and had to go by size.

When he got back to his room, he realized the shirt and trousers he'd stolen were both covered in a loud floral pattern.

Next morning at breakfast, he saw another guest wearing a floral outfit, and assumed it was the owner of the clothes he'd helped himself to. Rather than look the other way, he marched up to the man and accosted him.

'You may not know it yet,' he said angrily, 'but there's a laundry thief operating in this hotel, and he's asked me to pass a message on to you.'

The other guest frowned in confusion.

'A message… what message?'

'The message is this: "Please tell the man who wears absolutely atrocious floral clothes to go and buy something more neutral. And get a size bigger as well."'

The man in floral clothes balked.

'Why the hell should I get clothes to please the laundry thief?!'

Nasrudin regarded at the man obliquely.

'Don't ask me,' he retorted. 'I'm just the messenger.'

LANGLEY
VIRGINIA

Quadruple Agent

For years, Nasrudin was watched by the FBI, and was finally arrested for being a spy.

Day and night for a week, he was cross-questioned in a secret underground bunker.

Finally, he broke, and admitted to being a double agent.

The interrogator who was assigned to breaking the wise fool was about to turn off the recording equipment, when Nasrudin held up a hand.

'Actually,' he said softly, 'I'm a triple agent.'

'A *triple* agent?!'

The recording machine was switched back on, and Nasrudin explained how he had run missions undetected for decades.

At the end of the testimony, the recording equipment was shut down once again, and the officer gave the order for the prisoner to be returned to his cell.

'Actually,' Nasrudin said in a faint voice, 'I was a quadruple agent.'

'Quadruple agent?!' the interrogator balked. 'There's never been such a thing.'

'Not until now.'

Again, the machines were powered up and, again, the wise fool gave his testimony.

'Before we call it a day,' the officer snapped sarcastically, 'd'you want to tell me if there's anyone else up there in your head?'

Nasrudin raised his eyebrows.

'Possibly.'

'*Possibly*? What do you mean by that?'

'Well, it depends on who you think I am,' Nasrudin said.

EDINBURGH
SCOTLAND

Human Blinkers

Nasrudin observed that when he put blinkers on his donkey, the animal brayed less and worked harder.

One day, while idly going about his business, the thought of the blinkers and the donkey led through a zigzagging thought process to a revelation…

What if he were to market blinkers for humans, which would get them to gossip less and work more?

Days after having the idea, the wise fool made the first pair of blinkers, and tried them on himself. Although never diligent, he found that he was less distracted than before, and that the device caused him to talk less, too.

The blinkers went on sale.

Some sceptics railed against an invention they believed demeaned civil liberties, but the human blinkers were a triumphant success.

All over the world, employers bought the blinkers in their thousands and dished them out to their staff.

Overnight, global productivity soared.

Weeks passed, then calls rang out for another product to further increase concentration and output.

Once again, the wise fool thought long and hard.

And, by a series of coincidences, he came up with goggles that covered one eye with a patch and shrouded the other with an extra-harsh blinker.

Again, the innovation was a sensation.

Now a billionaire, Nasrudin was invited on TV.

'What are you working on as your next product?' the interviewer asked.

Over-excited at all the media attention, the wise fool rubbed his hands together.

'Next, we're going to launch blindfolds!' he snapped enthusiastically. 'After that, we'll release earplugs. And, after that, nose clamps, then gags. Once all these features are in place, we'll cover the worker's head in a kind of metal hood.'

The news anchor recoiled.

'If people can't see, hear, smell, or speak,' she gushed, 'how d'you expect them to do any work?'

'It's true they may be unable to work,' Nasrudin shot back, 'but just imagine how keen their concentration will be!'

SAN FRANCISCO
CALIFORNIA

Wise Fools Needed

While at a party in San Francisco, Nasrudin was once asked for his opinion on climate change.

'It's obvious to me,' he said, 'that climate change has come about because humans are unnecessarily intelligent.'

'What has intelligence got to do with climate change? Surely, it's the other way round – climate change occurring because humans are fools.'

'If our species wasn't so intelligent,' the wise fool clarified, 'it wouldn't continually question everything as it does. And, as a result, it would leave things alone.'

'Does that mean we'd be better off if everyone was a fool?' Nasrudin shrugged.

'We don't need fools or geniuses,' he replied.

'Then what *do* we need?'

'We need wise fools.'

TASHKENT

UZBEKISTAN

Up, Up, and Away!

While taking a stroll through the city's Victory Park, Nasrudin realized he was being followed by a large, fierce-looking dog.

Picking up his pace, he walked faster and faster.

But the dog did the same.

As the wise fool zigzagged through the park, the dog close on his heels, more dogs joined in.

Within a few minutes, the original dog was one in a pack of about fifty. Howling, snarling, and grimacing, the dogs seemed to be sizing the visitor up as their next meal.

Terrified, as he'd heard tales of ferocious Uzbek dogs tearing the innocent to pieces, Nasrudin tried to come up with a plan in order to give them the slip.

As he struggled to work out what to do, he spied a man selling helium balloons at the edge of the park.

He rushed over.

The dogs followed and clustered in a semi-circle, as if biding their time before they attacked.

Nasrudin picked out the largest balloon and paid for it.

Then, turning his back on the dogs, he took off his jacket and tied it to the balloon's string.

He let go.

The balloon floated gently up into the sky, taking the jacket with it.

Nasrudin turned to face the pack.

'Look! Look, you stupid mutts!' he shrieked. 'I'm floating up into the heavens! Catch me if you can!'

SHIRAZ
IRAN

Return to Sender

aving toured Iran for many weeks, Nasrudin had almost run out of funds, and didn't have any money for a flight home.

Fearful that he would overstay his visa, he went to the post office.

'How much would it cost to send a parcel weighing sixty-two kilogrammes to this address abroad?'

'Airmail or by sea?' the clerk asked.

'By air.'

'One thousand, four hundred and five rials.'

The wise fool counted his money.

'That's fine,' he said. 'I'll pay you now, and will leave the parcel outside the post office in an hour.'

Paying the money, Nasrudin hurried to the market, bought a crate large enough to fit into, and took it back to the post office.

In the shade of the building, he punctured some holes in the crate's sides, and slapped 'fragile' stickers on them.

Then he wrote his home details on the lid.

The pen, which had been lying in the sun, was leaking, and ink splattered all over the address.

With time against him, Nasrudin clambered into the crate and pleaded with a passer-by to nail down the lid.

'Are you sure?' the man asked.

The wise fool nodded.

Thinking he was doing a good deed, the passer-by did as he had been asked.

At that moment the post office porter heaved the crate onto his cart and, within the hour, it was in a van heading to their airport.

Inside the crate, Nasrudin beamed at having cheated the system yet again.

After one flight, and then another, the crate was off-loaded at a depot and loaded onto another van.

Having reached the province to which the crate was supposed to be delivered, the driver tried to read the name of the town – which was hidden under the ink-splatter.

'Looks like *Dalohan*…?' he muttered. 'Where on earth could that be?'

'*Taloqan*, you stupid fool!' Nasrudin yelled from the crate.

The driver began shaking.

'What kind of phantom are you?!'

'I'm not a phantom, you idiot! I'm simply a parcel that wants to get home to his family!'

Assuming he was hearing things as a result of working too hard, the driver took out a rubber stamp, spat on it, and slapped it down on the crate:

RETURN TO SENDER
ADDRESS UNKNOWN

TALLAHASSEE
FLORIDA

Boxed Experience

As a young man, Nasrudin had no experience, which meant he couldn't get a job – because employers would only take on staff with experience.

The wise fool had all but given up hope when, on his travels through the Deep South, he spied a little advertisement in a local newspaper.

The advert claimed to be selling 'boxes of experience'. As the price was reasonable, Nasrudin sent off his money and waited impatiently for the package to arrive.

Weeks passed. Then, one spring morning, a large box was delivered.

Overwhelmed with glee, the wise fool opened it.

Instead of the mass of papers and manuals he'd expected, he found a scrap of paper on which was written:

You have paid a fortune for this which proves you're desperate.

No, we didn't leave anything out, so there's no reason to complain.

When you ordered the box, you were raw and now you are ripe.

Next time you are asked for an example of your experience, explain about buying this box, and the lesson it taught you – and watch with wonder as the doors to your life open wide.

Feeling rather gypped at having spent so much money on such a small piece of advice, Nasrudin put it to the back of his mind and got on with his journey.

A few days passed. Then, one afternoon, he spotted another little advertisement in a newspaper. This time, it was searching for an intern to work for next to nothing in return for experience.

The advert didn't say what the job was. Intrigued, Nasrudin applied and was called for an interview. When asked for his experience, he explained about the box he had bought, the one containing the message.

'You've got the job,' the interviewer said firmly.

'Really?! Thank you!'

'Now, I'm sure you're wondering what the job is,' the manager said.

The wise fool nodded.

'We place adverts in newspapers offering boxes of experience at sky-high prices,' the interviewer told him. 'Your job will be making the boxes, putting the experience message inside, and shipping them out to people stupid enough to buy them.'

KOLKATA
INDIA

Desperate Times

Having shunned all material possessions, but not having received the largesse from a benefactor as he'd hoped, Nasrudin had no other choice but to take work as a *rickshawalla*.

He rented the ancient contraption and stood near the Oberoi Grand Hotel, waiting for a customer to hail him.

It wasn't long before a very large lady with a mountain of shopping called out.

When she had climbed aboard, the bags and parcels were heaved up into place on the passenger's lap.

Gritting his teeth, the wise fool grasped the handles and struggled to pull the rickshaw into the fray.

But he couldn't move it, not even a single inch.

Perched up on the seat, the customer offered a stream of insults.

'Even my husband's stronger than you,' she yelled, 'and he can't lift a feather!'

'Believe me, madam,' Nasrudin responded, 'I am pulling with all my strength.'

'Well, why can't you move it, then?!'

'Because "it" consists of the rickshaw, the shopping, and *you*!'

'If you knew yourself to be so scrawny, you shouldn't have taken a job as a *rickshawalla*!'

'Unfortunately, luck has been against me,' Nasrudin countered. 'And desperate times call for desperate measures, which is why I find myself standing here talking to you!'

EL-FAYOUM
EGYPT

Fault of the Student

hile searching for good camels for a journey across the desert, Nasrudin was directed to El-Fayoum, where the very best camels were said to be bought and sold.

It soon became clear that all the finest animals were owned by a miserly one-eyed dealer named Habib.

Despite bargaining hour after hour, the prices never went down.

In a bid to try a new tack, the wise fool tried to impress the merchant with stories of his adventures.

'One time I was stranded in the Thar Desert, and the local chief said he'd have me beheaded if I couldn't make him laugh. So, I did something no other man alive can do… I made my camels dance!'

Habib the camel dealer looked unimpressed.

'Don't believe it,' he grunted.

'But why not? It's absolutely true!'

Regarding the traveller with his single eye, Habib declared:

'If you can get any of my camels to dance, I'll give you whichever one you want for free.'

Next morning, Nasrudin picked a camel out from the herd, approached it slowly, and whispered in its ear. Then, staring deep into the animal's eye, he held up a forefinger and wagged it about.

An hour passed, but still the camel did not dance.

A second hour slipped by, in which Nasrudin grunted and groaned, and exchanged camels no less than five times.

Then, a third hour passed, with no sign of any dancing.

The only thing that happened, other than a crowd gathering as word of the dancing camels spread, was that a large male camel bit him on the ankle.

Infuriated, his pride severely dented, Nasrudin shook his fists in rage.

'What's the problem with your Egyptian camels?' he wailed. 'Camels in other countries are far better students than these!'

AGRA
INDIA

B-Movie

asrudin had managed to get a well-paid job for himself at the Taj Mahal, leading guided tours for American visitors.

One morning, while taking an especially large group of Californians to the mausoleum, he was overheard informing the visitors that the Taj Mahal had once been a pleasure palace to an ancient Aztec emperor.

'Picture the scene,' the wise fool said, 'jugglers, dancing girls, and courtesans, all of them here, and all of them from distant Mexico!'

The American visitors seemed confused.

'But everyone knows that the Taj was built as a burial place by the Mughal Emperor Shah Jehan for his beloved queen, Mumtaz Mahal,' one of them cried out.

Nasrudin winced, his eyes widening.

'You are Californians, are you not?'

Every head nodded.

'Well,' Nasrudin replied, 'as such, I assumed you'd want the B-movie version of history.'

KATHMANDU
NEPAL

It Is What It Is

Although a celebrated traveller, Nasrudin had a pitiable grasp of geography – a point which he tried to keep to himself as much as possible.

On a journey through Nepal, it came to the attention of a secondary school in the capital that the wise fool was visiting. The headteacher asked if he would take a break from his travels and teach geography for a term.

Flattered in a way he hadn't been flattered in a long time, the wise fool agreed, and was led to the class of teenagers awaiting him.

In the first lesson, he pointed to the large map of the world on the back wall of the classroom.

'Who can tell me what this place is?' he asked, pointing his baton at Australia.

'That's Australia, sir,' said a bright student at the front.

'Wrong!' he replied sternly. 'That is North America.'

Then, he pointed to North America and asked for its name.

A girl at the back put up her hand.

'North America, sir.'

'Wrong again!' Nasrudin called out. 'It's Africa!'

The process went on all afternoon, with the children calling out the right names, and their teacher insisting they were wrong.

Next day, the headteacher called the wise fool into his study.

'We have had complaints,' he said in a gruff voice. 'Some of your class complained to their parents, and they have complained to me.'

Fearful his lack of knowledge had been exposed, Nasrudin winced awkwardly.

'Who's to say what one place is and another is not?' he answered brightly.

The headteacher sighed.

'You were hired to teach geography,' he barked, 'not philosophy!'

MACAU
CHINA

Yamazamadooo!

n avid gambler, Nasrudin had been banned from all the casinos in Europe and the United States.

Fearing he would never be able to get to a gaming table again, he heard that Macau was so in need of gamblers that the territory never barred anyone.

Boarding a flight, he touched down at the airport and, within the hour, had taken his place at a splendid roulette wheel.

At first, all was well.

The wise fool handed over his money and was presented with a big stack of chips.

Then, placing them with care on the grid of numbers, he listened as the ball began to bounce around on the spinning roulette wheel.

As it slowed and clicked about, he thrust both arms above his head and yelled:

'Yamazamadooo! Yamazamadooo! Yamazamadooo!'

As if by magic, a butch-looking security guard appeared and ordered the gambler to cease his disturbance.

Nasrudin seemed glum.

'But without my little rituals,' he moaned, 'how am I ever expected to win?'

PARACAS
PERU

The Great White Shark

From the moment he'd swallowed the Komodo dragon, Nasrudin felt queasy and weak.

Indeed, the biliousness was unlike anything he had ever experienced. Even though he'd not experienced intestinal equilibrium since swallowing a bluebottle, the Komodo dragon had been the final straw.

And so, after consulting a backstreet oracle in the Indonesian capital, the wise fool travelled to the Peruvian coast and waited for a great white shark to put an end to all his problems.

As any scrawny example of humanity that's waited for a great white to find them knows, great whites are notoriously eager to feast on them.

Exactly a minute and a half after stepping into the water at Paracas, Nasrudin spied the dorsal fin of a great white zigzagging through the water towards him.

Ten seconds of silent trepidation followed.

Then, the moment of impact.

Now skilled in directing an advancing predator to his throat, Nasrudin swished to the side in the nick of time...

The great white shark hurtled into his mouth and was soon in his stomach.

Whooping with joy, the wise fool paddled out of the water. Once he was on the sand, he gave thanks to Providence, for ending the run of misfortune that had begun when he'd swallowed a bluebottle long, long before.

ASHKHABAD
TURKMENISTAN

Same Imagination

Since early childhood, Nasrudin had possessed an over-developed sense of imagination.

While the other children were playing out in the fields, he was sitting in his room, sketching intricate patterns. His parents feared their son would never make anything of himself, because all he could do was draw patterns.

Time passed.

One day, Nasrudin found a workshop in which Oriental carpets were being woven by a master craftsman. The expert showed off his stock to Nasrudin and demonstrated the way he took patterns from a sketchbook and conjured them into carpets.

Day after day, the wise fool would visit the master.

A little at a time, he learned the secret techniques of weaving the most intricate carpets ever made.

The years slipped by, and Nasrudin became a celebrated carpet-maker in his own right. Kings, queens, and presidents sought him out. However famous he became, the wise fool retained his sense of modesty, a point that went down well with the well-born and the rich.

Every year, Nasrudin's carpets became all the more intricate, while he himself appeared to be even more modest than before.

One day, he received a commission from the President of Turkmenistan. A fan of all things Turkmen, he completed the carpet, and travelled with it to the palace.

Unrolled in the throne room, Nasrudin's creation was admired by the president.

'I've never seen such astounding work!' he declared. 'Your imagination is really a thing of wonder.'

Bowing modestly, the wise fool blushed.

'It's really nothing,' he replied in little more than a whisper. 'In fact, it's less than nothing. I am ashamed to say that it's not my best work. Indeed, it's an utter abhorrence. If I were you, Mr. President, I would give the order for me to be clapped in irons, dragged to the dungeons, and tortured on a special machine used only to punish wayward carpet-makers like myself. Then, I'd have me flayed with canes made from the roots of monkey puzzle trees, and after that have me plunged into a vat of boiling bat vomit!'

The president looked at the carpet-maker in horror.

'Forgive me, sir,' whimpered Nasrudin. 'It's the same imagination that created the carpet getting the better of me again.'

RIYADH

SAUDI ARABIA

Selfish Courage

asrudin's life of adventure had seen him lauded as one of the most decorated military officials of his generation.

Having survived more campaigns than anyone could remember, he was frequently asked to speak to students all over the world. His lectures covered the subjects of war, peace and, most of all, courage.

At one event, a thousand school children packed into a large, air-conditioned auditorium. With rapt attention, they listened to the wise fool's address.

After much applause, a boy at the front raised his hand.

'Commander Nasrudin, I'd like to ask you what courage is.'

'I will tell you,' the soldier replied in a flash. 'Courage is selfishness.'

'What do you mean, sir?' the child called back.

'Well, if I was to die in battle,' Nasrudin elucidated, 'the man next to me would get my rations. That is a state of affairs I would not wish to happen. Rather, I want him to get killed so I can get my hands on *his* rations.'

'So, the courage that's been responsible for making you a war hero was all down to hoping for extra rations of food?'

Nasrudin frowned awkwardly.

'Some things in life are wonderful when considered from close up,' he said, 'but far less attractive when viewed at a distance.'

NYAUNG OHAK
MYANMAR

Honest Bait

Nasrudin had been exploring the ancient temple structures at Nyaung Ohak, overgrown as they were with foliage, creepers and vines.

Just as he was about to make his way back to the path, he spotted the most beautiful butterfly with iridescent wings soaking up the sun on the branch of a tree.

With great care, he approached.

'Stay there so I can catch you,' he whispered.

To his surprise, the insect answered back:

'So you can stick a pin through me, fix me to a board, put me in a frame, and hang me on a wall?'

'No, no, no,' Nasrudin stammered. 'I promise it wouldn't be like that!'

The butterfly let out a grunt.

'Then what would you do with me?'

'I'd take you back to my country and…'

'*And…?*'

'And keep you as a pet.'

'That's a lie!'

'No it's not.'

'Yes, it is, and we both know it!'

'OK OK! You're right! It's a lie!' Nasrudin admitted. 'But how am I expected to catch anything with the truth?'

DAMASCUS
SYRIA

Knowing Your Ways

Nasrudin flew into Damascus in the middle of the night and was horrified to find that his suitcase was not waiting for him at the carousel.

Undeterred, he simply grabbed someone else's luggage, making sure that it bore the same general look. The way he figured it, anyone with a suitcase like his would have the same clothes.

From the airport, the wise fool took a taxi to Bab Tooma and made his way to the guesthouse he had booked. Once in his room, he put the case on the bed and opened it up.

To his surprise, the luggage was filled with terribly inferior clothes, none of which fitted him. Incensed that he had been put out so badly, Nasrudin fumbled for the luggage label and saw there was a phone number given.

He dialled the number.

'How dare you have such terrible taste!' he yelled.

'Who is this?' said a concerned voice on the other end.

'I'm the person who took your suitcase. *Why?* Well, it's obvious… I couldn't see my case, so I took yours. After all, it's just about the same size and colour as mine.'

The owner of the case was about to launch into an attack and demand his luggage back, when Nasrudin cut him off:

'I can't believe you expected me to deal with such rotten clothing as yours! It's a disgrace!'

There was silence for a moment, while the man at the other end registered what was happening.

'How the hell can you be complaining?!' he screamed. 'After all, you're the thief who stole my case!'

'I have every right to complain,' bellowed Nasrudin.

'No you don't!'

'Yes I do!'

'How on earth could you reason that?' the owner of the suitcase yelled.

'Because if the tables were turned… and it was you who stole my case… I'd expect you to complain to me.'

'Wait a minute… You're complaining because you think I would have complained?'

'Yes,' sniffed Nasrudin.

The rightful owner of the case could hardly speak, such was his rage.

'How the hell d'you know what I would do in the circumstances?! You don't even know me!'

Nasrudin cast an eye over the belongings that were not his.

'Maybe I didn't know you at the start of the call,' he answered icily, 'but I've got a pretty firm idea now of what you're like!'

DOHA
QATAR

Different Luck

Nasrudin had learned from a local magazine that a fortune could be made in the oil fields of Qatar.

A prospector at heart, he dropped everything, flew to the desert emirate, and arrived at the Oil Ministry.

The official in charge took his paperwork, then asked how much land he intended to acquire for the search for oil.

'Three square feet should do me,' Nasrudin replied brightly.

The clerk balked.

'Are you out of your mind?'

'Perhaps,' the wise wool responded, 'but I hardly think it has a bearing on my current activity.'

'How do you expect to have any luck in discovering natural reserves in such a tiny plot of land?'

Nasrudin shrugged.

'It may be a small area to you,' he responded snootily, 'but in my family we're blessed with a different kind of luck.'

INTERLAKEN
SWITZERLAND

Enthusiastic Ignorance

The great and the good had arrived in the Swiss Alps for the World Yodelling Championships.

Most of the participants had been drawn from nearby valleys.

A few had travelled from other cantons.

But none had journeyed as far as the champion of champions, the wise fool, Nasrudin.

The judges couldn't understand how a participant, who claimed only to have started yodelling three months before while taking a bath, had excelled in quite such spectacular style.

Once the awards ceremony was over, one of the other yodellers asked Nasrudin for his technique.

'My technique,' he answered in bewilderment, 'is nothing more than enthusiastic ignorance!'

MEKELLE
ETHIOPIA

Rain Machine

n a zigzagging journey through Ethiopia, Nasrudin finally reached the capital of the northern Tigray region.

He had eaten a huge lunch of *doro wot* and was sitting on a bench on Alula Street. As he sat there digesting his lunch, a pigeon flew under the bench and started flapping about.

In what was an instinctive reaction, he reached down and tried to shoo the bird away.

His hand swishing about under the bench, the fingers brushed against something unexpected...

What felt like a plastic object.

Curious as to what it could be, he got down on his knees and peered under the bench. To his surprise, he saw that a large button had been fixed to the underside of the bench with duct tape. It was the kind of button used in factories to turn machinery on and off.

Pulling it away, he sat back on the bench and looked at it closely.

There was no writing on the unit, except a pair of words in capitals:

ON, OFF.

Intrigued, Nasrudin pressed the button.

Nothing happened. Not at first...

But then... a minute or two later, it started to rain.

Thrilled with his discovery, the wise fool concluded that the button was a remote control for the weather. As there were no settings other than the switch, he assumed it was a model that did no more than make it rain, or make the rain stop.

Sitting, rain lashing down, he decided to test whether the button could turn the rain off as well as turn it on.

So he pressed the button a second time.

Again, nothing happened at first.

But, a minute or two later, the rain shower ceased.

'Excellent!' Nasrudin thought to himself. 'This little button can help the farmers of Ethiopia.'

Next day, while continuing his travels southwards on the long journey towards Addis Ababa, he passed a farm – little more than a patch of land cleared of stones.

In the middle of the field, a farmer was ploughing the ground with a weary-looking ox, beneath an empty sky – cloudless and blue.

Buoyed by his discovery the day before, Nasrudin strode over and called greetings.

'When did it last rain here?' he asked the farmer.

'A long time ago,' came the reply.

'Well, how would you feel if I could make it rain right now?'

The farmer's eyes lit up.

'I'd be a very happy man,' he answered.

Like a magician preparing to execute a trick, the wise fool took the plastic button from his backpack and held it up.

'I'm about to change your life,' he said.

'What's that?' the farmer asked suspiciously.

'It's a magic button that makes it rain.'

The farmer gasped at the thought.

Then Nasrudin smiled. As he did so, he pressed the button – turning on the rain.

Nothing happened.

'We may have to wait a minute or two,' the wise fool explained. 'Sometimes it needs time to warm up.'

So they waited.

Still nothing.

Nasrudin pressed again, and again. After that he shook the button.

'Sorry about that,' he said dejectedly, 'the batteries must need changing.'

BUCHAREST
ROMANIA

Ridiculous Rock

While walking down the street in Bucharest, Nasrudin tripped over a rock and broke his big toe.

In considerable pain, he hobbled to the nearest hospital and asked for an X-ray to be done.

After an hour of waiting, a doctor saw to him.

'Do you have health insurance?' he asked.

The wise fool shook his head.

'No, I don't, doctor. But, since I tripped over a rock in the street, and it was the rock's fault, the offending rock will be paying for my treatment.'

The doctor burst out laughing at the thought of a rock paying for anything.

'I don't know what you find so funny,' Nasrudin answered indignantly.

'Well, it's a ridiculous idea – that a rock would have money to pay for hospital treatment.'

Nasrudin regarded the physician icily.

'You mean as ridiculous an idea as leaving a rock lying about for the innocent to trip over?'

GOLSPIE
SCOTLAND

Right to Be Wrong

Nasrudin adored the Highlands, which reminded him of his own homeland.

He'd often visit his old friend the Laird Hamish McDonnell, and the two of them would swap stories of clans, of traditions, and of adventure.

On one visit to the laird, Nasrudin was overcome with emotion.

'I love it here so much,' he said, his eyes welling with tears, 'that I never want to travel anywhere else again!'

McDonnell took a sip of his whisky.

'You say that every time you come here, Nasrudin.'

'I know I do,' the wise fool answered, 'but this time I really mean it.'

'Do you?'

'Yes. But, even if I don't, it's my right to be wrong.'

LISBON
PORTUGAL

The Path to Celebrity

N asrudin went into a shop, bought an iPhone, and smashed it on the ground.

Then, he went back into the same shop, bought another iPhone, went outside, and smashed it, too.

After that, he broke another iPhone, and another, and another.

Within an hour, a crowd had gathered. Everyone was asking in raised voices why anyone would be so crazy as to smash perfectly good, brand-new iPhones.

Nasrudin didn't reply.

Instead, he kept going into the shop, buying iPhones, and smashing them outside.

That evening, the national news channel sent a reporter and film crew to interview him, as the crowd swelled to ten thousand people.

The entire country was obsessed with the reason why anyone would act in such a strange way. Despite the media frenzy surrounding him, Nasrudin wouldn't reveal the reason.

After three days of smashing iPhones, a national newspaper offered to pay a million euros for an exclusive on why he was doing what he was doing.

Taking the fee, which more than covered the cost of the phones, he agreed he was at last ready to answer questions.

'Tell us, why have you broken so many new iPhones?' the reporter asked.

'Simple,' Nasrudin answered, 'I was turning myself from one thing into another.'

'Can you explain what you mean?'

The wise fool nodded.

'Three days ago I was a normal member of the public,' he replied. 'But now I'm a mere mortal no longer.'

'Then what are you?'

'A celebrity.'

FÈS
MOROCCO

Feast of Imagination

Nasrudin had no money with which to buy lunch for his guests.

So, when they arrived at his house, he made an announcement:

'Unfortunately, the bazaar was closed today,' he lied, 'so we are having a special kind of meal instead.'

'What kind of meal?' one of the guests asked, her curiosity piqued.

'A Feast of Imagination.'

Once the guests were shown to their seats, the wise fool passed around a host of dishes.

First, he pointed to a little patterned bowl containing gravel.

'These are olives,' he said.

Next, he motioned to a large terracotta platter filled with black pebbles.

'And this one's a delicious lamb tagine,' he said.

Finally, he pointed out a tureen filled with cold water at the edge of the table.

'That's a mouth-watering soup,' he said, 'made with my mother's recipe.'

Assuming their host was having a joke at their expense, one of the guests stormed out.

A second pretended she liked the pebble tagine.

A third, who was Nasrudin's equal in terms of intellect, or rather the lack of it, held up a little vase of flowers.

'Can we pretend this is the dessert?' she asked cheerily.

The wise fool was overjoyed.

'Yes!' he exclaimed. 'It's a special chocolate mousse, which I made myself!'

MUNICH
GERMANY

Advanced Warning

Nasrudin bought the latest generation of phone which could be folded into the size of a matchbox.

While showing off the technology to his friends, he got over-excited, put the device in his mouth – and swallowed it by mistake.

Bereft at losing his phone, the wise fool went to the local hospital.

The doctor listened to what had happened.

'The danger of it tearing your internal organs is very great,' he said. 'We have no choice but to cut you open.'

His eyes welling with tears at the thought of surgery, Nasrudin asked the doctor if he could borrow his phone.

'Yes, of course,' the physician answered. 'D'you want to phone your family and tell them of the operation?'

'No,' the wise fool responded. 'I want to call my stomach and tell it to get ready for the knife.'

KRAKÓW
POLAND

Underwear Song

Nasrudin was singing a beautiful lilting song on a tram one morning, his mind far away.

By chance, a music producer was riding in the same carriage, and overheard the song.

It was the most beautiful thing he'd heard in years.

The next thing Nasrudin knew, he'd been signed to a major record label and the song had become an international sensation.

Invited on a leading Polish chat show, the wise fool was asked what the mysterious words in the song actually meant.

Nasrudin blushed.

'Nothing of consequence,' he replied tautly.

'Oh, but the main lyric must have a meaning,' the interviewer asked for a second time.

'Yes, it does.'

'Well, I'm sure all your fans out there want to know its meaning.'

His face the colour of a ripe tomato, the wise fool whispered:

'It means: "Oh I must remember to change my underpants when I get home tonight!"'

LOS ANGELES
CALIFORNIA

Cat Think

Nasrudin won an old tortoiseshell cat in a raffle and, although her pernickety ways bothered him, the wise fool grew to love the animal.

He would spend hours each day making delicious meals for his pet, and tempting her to eat just a little of the food he'd prepared.

One day, while trying to make the cat jealous, he took a tiny bite of her food. To his surprise, it was absolutely mouth-watering. That afternoon, while his beloved cat dozed on the sofa, Nasrudin had an idea.

Why not make the world's first brand of cat food for humans?

Without wasting a moment, that's exactly what he did.

Within weeks, the meals were a sensation with cat-lovers everywhere. Soon, he'd branched off to make a range of dog food for dog-lovers, and then human food for cats and for dogs.

A year after starting the lucrative business venture, Nasrudin was snuggling on the sofa with his now-famous pet.

'The source of my wealth all came about because you wouldn't do as I'd asked you and eat your food,' he cooed. 'As a reward, I'll give you anything you like.'

At that moment, the feline let out a sharp meow, as if indicating she wanted to curl up on her owner's favourite blanket.

'You're a genius, my dear!' Nasrudin yelled. 'I'll make cat blankets for people and people blankets for cats!'

Again, the idea was a runaway success.

A few weeks later, when the product launches were over, the wise fool cuddled his beloved cat again.

'I'll never get over how you send me these ideas telepathically,' he whispered. 'And, to think of it, I never even learned to understand Spoken Cat.'

TANNA
VANUATU

A Higher Power

O n a military training exercise, Nasrudin made a high-altitude freefall jump and, missing the deck of the aircraft carrier he was aiming for, parachuted onto the small island of Tanna.

While trying to work out what had gone wrong and how he had ended up on the remote island in the South Pacific, the local tribespeople rushed from the undergrowth and proclaimed him to be their living god.

'You fell from the sky, O Great One!' they cried.

'Yes, I parachuted from high altitude, but seem to have missed the ship that's waiting for me,' the wise fool explained.

'You'll live with us here on Tanna, and we will worship you!' the populace cried.

'Alas, I have to leave now.'

The chief shook his head.

'You can never leave, because we've waited centuries for you.'

'I'm flattered,' Nasrudin replied, 'but even though I may be your god, I myself answer to a higher power.'

'What is the name of the Greatest God?' the chief asked urgently.

'The Greatest God is named "Sergeant Major".'

SWEETWATER
TEXAS

The Bluebottle

ith the great white shark inside him, Nasrudin could at last relax.

Having celebrated long into the night, he made his way from the Peruvian seaboard, up through Central America, into Mexico, then across into Texas.

Zigzagging northwards, he found himself sitting on the very same park bench where his troubles had begun, lunchbox in hand.

As he raised a sandwich to his lips, Nasrudin felt tautness in his stomach.

Tautness that led to a pang of jabbing pain.

He burped no ordinary burp.

But a burp so violent that it seemed to shake the bench, and then the ground.

In a reflex well beyond his control, the great white shark from the Peruvian waters gushed out of his mouth.

Then, the Komodo dragon was ejected.

After it, the black panther.

And the aardvark.

Fifty thousand termites followed.

After them came the polar bear.

Once it had romped from Nasrudin's throat, the snow leopard leapt out.

Next, the reticulated python.

Then, the tiger from the Sunderbans.

And the laughing hyena.

Arms flailing, the blue-ringed octopus emerged.

After it was the banded mongoose.

Then, the sewer rat from Mumbai's subterranean realm.

And the pink-toed tarantula.

As the wise fool gasped for breath, the bluebottle buzzed out into the light.

His eyes wide and reeling from such a monumental bout of disgorging, Nasrudin gave thanks to his ancestors for having returned him to a state of normality.

Lifting the sandwich to his lips, he prepared to take a bite… But, as he did so, a large bluebottle with iridescent wings flew into his mouth and down his throat.

Nasrudin groaned, cursed, and cried out:

'Here we go again!'

PAGHMAN
AFGHANISTAN

Chicken and Egg

asrudin paid in advance for six chickens and was given a box of half a dozen eggs.

Furious, he complained to the butcher, who was a conman.

Hoping to get his own back, he offered to sell the man a hundred loaves of bread for a hundred afghanis.

'I bet you're just going to give me a handful of wheat!' the butcher hissed.

'How did you know?' the wise fool grumbled, tossing away the grain.

'I know because I invented that trick!'

A week went by, and still Nasrudin wanted to get revenge.

Then, as if by magic, he had an idea.

First, he went to the teahouse when he knew the butcher would be there. Once inside, he cajoled another fool to spread the word that a chicken from Paghman, that laid golden eggs, had been found in Kabul.

Next day, Nasrudin painted gold the six eggs from the week before and bought a live chicken in the market.

Ambling over to the butcher's, Nasrudin got chatting to a friend outside.

Always curious what the wise fool was up to, the friend asked where he was going with the chicken and the egg box.

Nasrudin cupped a hand to his friend's ear and whispered:

'I know I can trust you, so I'll tell you, and you alone.'

'Tell me what?'

'The most remarkable thing. You see, last week, that butcher in the shop behind us sold me some eggs. Only one of them hatched. In a single day it grew to a full-size bird. And then, in a single night it laid half a dozen eggs. But they're no ordinary eggs… they're gold!'

Opening the box, the wise fool showed the eggs off.

'What are you going to do with them?' the friend asked.

'Well, I'm waiting for someone who works in the ministry to collect me and take me to meet the governor. As an honest member of society, I think it only fit that the chicken and the eggs are shared out with all the people of Paghman.'

Amazed, the friend slipped into the butcher's shop and, a moment later, the conman hurried out.

'Dearest Nasrudin!' he roared. 'I think I sold you one of the defective chickens in egg form last week. I do apologize!'

'You mean, the amazing chicken-egg that grew overnight, and has now blessed me with a life of golden eggs?'

'Yes, yes, the very same,' the butcher gushed, taking a look at the creature.

The wise fool opened the egg box and showed off the eggs.

'Well, I can only thank you from the bottom of my heart!' Nasrudin crooned. 'For the chicken is a blessing for all the people of Paghman. I'm taking her to the governor.'

The butcher's face froze.

'But, surely, as it's a defective chicken there is a health risk to consider,' he said. 'And, as the man who sold you the egg, I ought to take responsibility and try and get to the bottom of what occurred.'

Nasrudin slipped the conman a sideways glance.

'But the lovely little creature is laying eggs like these in abundance – at least six a day! She's sure to make us all rich!'

His heart pounding at the thought of such wealth, the butcher held up a thick wad of money.

'Let me buy her right now,' he begged.

'On one condition,' Nasrudin replied.

'Which is?'

'That you take the chicken and your family, and leave Paghman by dusk.'

The money and the bird changed hands.

The eggs were cracked and made into a delicious omelette.

The story was told and retold in the teahouse for weeks.

As for the butcher, he was never seen again.

WIMBLEDON
ENGLAND

We Know Differently

aving secured himself a well-positioned seat on the Centre Court, Nasrudin took his place and watched as the players warmed up.

A few minutes later, the two top-seeded players stepped out.

Beside himself with excitement, the wise fool kept on clapping for no reason at all.

It wasn't long before an official ordered him to be silent for fear of being thrown out.

Nasrudin piped down for a while.

But then, once again, the excitement became too much for him.

'Look! There! A ball's coming at you!' he screeched.

Nasrudin was given an extremely stern rebuke, but promised to be as good as gold.

A minute later, though, he yelled out:

'There! There! Watch out!'

As the wise fool was being dragged out of his seat, he asked what all the fuss was about.

'You're disturbing play!' the officer snarled.

'That's what *you* may think,' he riposted. 'But the racquets and I know differently!'

GLASGOW
SCOTLAND

Yes Man

A legendary media mogul was so insecure that his chief of staff frequently hired 'yes men' to agree with whatever he said.

As the position was so limited in terms of duties, and so badly paid, candidates were few and far between.

With no other job prospects on the horizon, Nasrudin saw the advertisement for the job of Yes Man and applied.

At the interview he was briefed on what was expected of him.

'You'll sit in on meetings,' the chief of staff explained, 'and if the CEO asks you anything at all, just agree and say, "Yes, sir!" at the top of your lungs. D'you understand?'

The wise fool gave a double thumbs up.

'Yes, sir!' he beamed.

'I think you'll do well here,' the chief of staff said.

Next day, Nasrudin sat in on his first meeting. After what seemed like ages, the CEO turned to him.

'Are you the new man called Smith?'

'Yes, sir!'

'Do you like my policies, Smith?'

'Yes, sir!'

The CEO seemed pleased.

'Tell me, Smith, I heard a rumour that people out there are saying I'm stupid and fat... D'you think they're right, Smith?'

'Yes, sir!'

'You're fired, Smith! Get out!'

'Yes, sir!'

PORTO
PORTUGAL

Constructive Spooking

Even as an adult, Nasrudin was terrified of the monster he was certain lived under his bed.

One night, plucking up courage, he peered under the bed in which he was lying, and gasped because there was no monster there.

Rather than calming down, the wise fool was overcome with anger.

'Don't think you can go invisible on me!' he thundered. 'We both know you're there!'

Still, there was silence.

'If you're so good at making yourself invisible,' Nasrudin roared, 'why don't you go and use your spooking skills for something constructive instead of terrifying people like me?!'

MAZAR-I-SHARIF
AFGHANISTAN

No Cupboard for Skeletons

asrudin was so dyslexic he couldn't spell his own name, and left school without any qualifications at all.

After trying to land a series of dead-end jobs without any luck, he found employment cleaning out toilets in a public building. Respectful to others by nature, he did well in tips.

The customers who used the toilets liked that he was there when needed to hand them a towel or soap, but that he kept out of their way.

One day, while trudging around cleaning the cubicles, two well-dressed men entered the washroom.

As they seemed to be searching for a quiet place to speak, Nasrudin slipped into one of the stalls and listened.

The first man clapped his hands together in anger.

'The governor's an absolute imbecile!' he ranted.

'So let's put another man in the job,' the other man replied.

'Of course that would suit us both, but who could we get to take that godforsaken job?'

'Surely, no one.'

'We need someone who's polite but who won't get in our way.'

'Yes... a man who is meek but who has a past. We both know that anyone seeking to be a governor always has to have skeletons in their cupboards.'

As the two men talked, Nasrudin crept out of the cubicle and into the hallway. Helping himself to an overcoat and a hat from the rack, he waited.

As soon as the well-dressed men emerged from the washroom, he rushed up.

'Gentlemen!' he exclaimed, embracing them. 'I do hope I am not late!'

'Who are you?' the men said at once.

'The replacement.'

'*Replacement?*'

'Yes, indeed.'

'The replacement for *what?*'

'For governor of course!'

The men exchanged a troubled glance. The thought of being found out for scheming was terrifying. Plucking up courage, one spoke for both:

'How d'you know that the appointment of a new governor was on the cards?'

The wise fool smiled demurely.

'As a man of discretion,' he answered, 'it is not for me to know. That's why the president asked me to travel here from Kabul and make myself available.'

'You know the President of the Republic?'

Nasrudin smiled again meekly.

'His last words to me were "Don't forget to tell them that you're a man who doesn't own any skeletons, let alone a cupboard to put them in!"'

ROOSVILLE
CANADA

Used Air Business

Day in, day out, Nasrudin would cross the border from Canada to the United States at Roosville.

Whenever he traversed, he was found to be holding a large, empty glass jar.

Each day, the officials on either side of the frontier ordered him to declare any valuables or contraband.

'I've only got this worthless glass jar,' he would say each time. 'It's filled with nothing but air.'

Even though the officials knew the answer he would give, they quizzed him on the jar's contents.

'Used air,' Nasrudin would say each time. 'I'm in the used air business.'

One day, the customs agent on the Canadian side of the border winked at the wise fool.

'D'you really expect me to believe that?'

'No, officer,' Nasrudin replied.

'Then why d'you say it day after day, month after month?'
'Because if you knew the truth, you'd arrest me.'
'What for?'
'Selling used air without a licence.'

VILNIUS
LITHUANIA

Quick Think

Nasrudin was caught by a neighbour taking a short cut through his garden.

The man had warned Nasrudin a hundred times to go the long way round – which meant another forty minutes of walking each way.

'Oh, but I'm not sneaking through your land as you think I am,' he said.

'What are you doing here then?'

'I was looking for you, actually.'

'What for?'

'To make you a business offer.'

'What is it?'

'To ask if you wanted to buy my cat.'

'To hell with you, I hate cats! I don't want to buy *any* cat, let alone yours!' the angry neighbour answered with characteristic ire.

'Are you quite sure?'

'What a strange thing to ask… whether I want to buy your cat! It's the very worst example of a business deal I've ever heard!'

'Perhaps,' Nasrudin answered tautly, 'but it's the very best example of Quick Think *I've* ever heard!'

TOKYO
JAPAN

Artificial Unintelligence

asrudin spent all his money in the Akihabara technology district on a robot with AI named Blinkie.

The salesman at the electronics shop promised it would do all the respected customer's thinking for him.

Following a complex set-up procedure, the wise fool told Blinkie everything about himself, so that he would think just like he did.

A day and night of pandemonium came and went, at the end of which the wise fool took Blinkie back to the shop in a fluster.

'I want my money back!' he thundered.

The salesman enquired why.

'The reason I bought this damned robot was to have some intelligence in the house… the last thing I wanted was another imbecile like me!'

Finis

THE
MYSTIFYING
MISADVENTURES
OF
THE
MYSTIFYING
NASRUDIN

TAHIR SHAH

THE
PEREGRINATIONS
OF THE
PERPLEXING
NASRUDIN

TAHIR SHAH

TRAVELS
WITH
NASRUDIN

TAHIR SHAH

A REQUEST

If you enjoyed this book, please review it on your favourite online retailer or review website.

Reviews are an author's best friend.

To stay in touch with Tahir Shah, and to hear about his upcoming releases before anyone else, please sign up for his mailing list:

 http://tahirshah.com/newsletter

And to follow him on social media, please go to any of the following links:

 http://www.twitter.com/humanstew

 @tahirshah999

 http://www.facebook.com/TahirShahAuthor

 http://www.youtube.com/user/tahirshah999

 http://www.pinterest.com/tahirshah

 https://www.goodreads.com/tahirshahauthor

http://www.tahirshah.com